Elysian Fields

Elysian Fields

Twila Gingerich

For A and N.

And for those who lost their growing up years surviving the unsurvivable.

Contents

I

A small square of sunlight gently appeared on the floor, the sun's first appearance of the day. It glimmered ivory white near my feet for a moment, hesitated, and then withdrew, shutting itself up in the sky again.

As a mentally ill person, I had many appointments. There were routine checkup appointments, emergency booked-as-needed appointments, goodbye-and-a-referral appointments.

The sun was wavering over an initial evaluation appointment that day.

"How long did those feelings last for?" asked the counsellor. She sat opposite me, soft-faced, her narrow shoulders framed by the taut leather of a tall-backed chair. Her name was Sonya and her counselling office was in a large, square room, nestled in the east end of a distinguished modern home. Harsh, clear lines in the middle of an unkempt forest.

"Hard to say." I put myself back in time to remember. Cool, grey tile beneath my feet, black evening sky outside the windows, cement in my lungs, death seizing in my heart. My thirteen-year-old face blanched and frozen in the bathroom mirror. "I think about fifteen minutes. No more than twenty."

Sonya's small hand wrote down what I had said. Her eyes moved toward the clock. "I see that we're coming to the end of our hour here, but I just want to complete this thought. It was at

1

the age of thirteen that you first experienced suicidal thoughts. You had these thoughts during a panic attack, and you stayed in the bathroom until the panic attack passed, which was about fifteen or twenty minutes."

The beginning of my mental illness was summarized nicely, neat like a tiny square gift box, a pink silk ribbon tied into place.

I glanced around the room as Sonya consulted her notes. Her voice was smooth, like warm molasses. Her warmth did not make sense against the cold, white walls and dark furniture, yet her lifetime of possessions was anything but impersonal. The home was a small factory of books, amateur photographs, chipped keepsakes, magazines that had lost their gloss. Wooden wind chimes were decidedly hung indoors; a small marble elephant sat on a tall stack of psychoanalysis books.

"Did the suicidal thoughts persist once you first experienced them?" My attention was drawn back to Sonya as she spoke.

"All throughout my teenage years," I answered, stopping short, as if my twentieth birthday had barred the suicidal thoughts from following me.

"I see," said Sonya, nodding and writing in unison. "You thought about death quite a lot while you were still very young."

I had. Most days were like a wet wool blanket wrapped around my head. Suffocating—not dying—only suffocating. Wanting to either get the blanket off or suffocate entirely.

The appointment had come to a close. The first was always the hardest, like wading into an ice-cold stream, the shock of cold inching up the body until full submersion. I had forced truths through my teeth even when I wanted to sugarcoat every word to soften its severity. Sonya had been the scribe while I spoke. My words were written down and had now evaporated into the air.

As I put on my coat to leave, a faint tapping echoed behind me.

"I will see you next week, Imogen." Sonya picked off a dead leaf from a spider plant that consumed the little table it sat on.

The tapping continued and became louder until a dog's polite face appeared in the doorway. A small stab of joy hit my heart.

"Oh, yes," said Sonya, "I meant to ask this before. Are you comfortable with dogs?"

"Of course." I kept my eyes on the dog, avoiding eye contact with Sonya. "What's their name?"

"That's Forest," said Sonya. The mention of their name instantly sped up Forest's approach. A Labrador, espresso brown, save for the feathers of grey around their snout and eyes. Smile lines. "She's a little older. I try to let her be around me as much as I can. She attends many of my counselling sessions as well." Sonya ran her hand over Forest's head. "But never the first appointment. You need to meet her and decide if you would mind her being in the room."

"Of course I don't mind." It was preferred.

"Beautiful. You will see her next week as well then."

Forest's heart-shaped face looked on after me until the door closed behind my back.

I drove down the long driveway that was a tunnel through overhanging white oak trees. There was always a fatigue after therapy that settled into my bones and fastened to them for the rest of that day. I looked forward to my bed.

Sonya lived in the northeast corner of the city, on land that, until recently, had been fields of wheat and soybeans. Farmland had been cut up neatly like a sheet cake and sold, and the city slowly spilled out, continuously reaching outside of its limits. I drove into the city from the outskirts, watching it grow denser until I arrived at my apartment.

Monday morning came as a cold north wind ran rampant through the city's street veins. I poured coffee into a mug. The mug had been my grandfather's; he had brought it home with him after a trip to Guyana, and I had loved it so much as a child, always asking for my morning orange juice to be poured into it. He gifted the mug to me one Christmas.

I sat down and looked into the dark abyss of black coffee. The kitchen light reflected on its surface, a little pool of white in the middle of the cup. I thought I would feel a sense of accomplishment being in my last term of university, the chequered flag in full view. Soon, I would be slipping into the adult world. Instead, time slowed down, becoming heavy and monotonous. I would sweep the floor only for it to get dirty, refill the gas tank only for it to empty, watch the cars like ants following one another in a mindless procession. People scurried around like field mice. We were collectively in a dream trying to run, but it was the kind of dream in which our legs didn't move as they should, and we would never arrive.

The prospect of graduation turned grey: an accomplishment near the beginning of a long list of required accomplishments.

Classes were attended and courses completed until I had climbed my way into year four. For four years, I had run to and fro between campus buildings, an amalgamation of new and old design. Original brown-bricked buildings on the east side, glass and steel buildings increasingly moving west.

On Monday evenings, the heavy metal doors of the oldest lecture hall on campus swallowed me whole. Reality warped and time slowed within those walls. I could count on one hand now the number of classes left for me to attend in the building.

I slipped into a back-row seat of the lecture hall, ever intent on obscuring the gaze of whosoever looked my way. Damp air permeated the room, brought in by each student as they stepped out of the cold outdoors, where the north wind blew over snow and frozen waters. I reached for my phone in the quiet before class and texted my boyfriend Jesse to let him know I had entered the fifth circle of hell and was just waiting for the professor to join. It had become a habit to order my courses in descending order from most to least favourite, and I would call them by their respective numbers in the circle of hell as outlined in Dante's *Inferno*. Starting with the fifth circle and ending with the final ninth circle, the most accursed circle, I could tell Jesse how good or bad of a school day it was. After two years of dating, I'd realized he would never remember a course in the program I was taking, so I had found a method that worked.

I sent the text at six in the evening, yet Jesse would be receiving it at three in the afternoon. Jesse lived three hours behind me, working for an environmental company in British Columbia.

Jesse had no fixed compass; sometimes he looked like a free spirit, other times he looked merely adrift.

But for the time being, he found himself in the middle of nowhere B.C., passing joints around the circle of homely environmentalists, fire pit in the eye of the storm, earthy marijuana smoke joining ashy campfire smoke in the sky.

Half our relationship had been long distance, but Jesse would fly back home every couple of months to see me and his mom, brother, and sister. I didn't mind the time apart. It kept me independent and not altogether consumed by the artificial bubble of dating life.

Jesse had texted back: *Good luck, kid.*

Ms. Sardinha walked down the long aisle to the front of the classroom at exactly six thirty. She was rarely early, never late, and always prepared to start her lecture as soon as she got to the front of the class. The middle-aged Brazilian woman was prim, timely, organized, and impartial, if not cold at times. I admired her immensely.

I had sat through hundreds of lectures, but my mind often failed to follow the progression of information. Ms. Sardinha would explain a concept, and my brain would get snagged on a single sentence or thought and would play it again and again like a skipping record, my OCD working overtime for several seconds until something snapped, and I would have to struggle to catch up with what the professor was saying in real-time.

I had tentatively begun university at the age of twenty, two years later than the prescribed timeline. I stepped into the current and the undertow washed me up on the other side of the river in the final term of the fourth year, mere weeks away from touching the mirage that had been weakly glinting in the distance.

My existence as a university student was a minor miracle. The tangled history of my academic record would not lead one to believe I would achieve post-secondary. I found it quite funny that I held the esteemed label of *university student* when I knew the patchwork quilt of schooling that loosely held together my education. Public school classrooms, nervous breakdowns, wondering how to make a heart permanently stop beating, homeschooling years, attempts of reentering the brick-and-mortar school buildings, failing in the outside world, enrolling in online courses, trips to the academic advisor, trips to the hospital, boarding school considerations. My parents had wondered what would become of me by high school's end. But I kept moving forward because that was the only direction I could move in, and I graduated. I applied to schools I was terrified of attending, and I was accepted by some and enrolled in one.

But others' tales of high school memories—the parties, the classes skipped—would always cause a strange smile, cold and demure, to appear on my face. When those memories ricocheted in campus hallways between classes, I would nod and pretend I had lived the same life. I didn't say much. They didn't ask much.

I made one good friend in university, or rather someone had befriended me and brought me into their fold. This was Miyu. Small and high-functioning, she was both studious and a partier, and she had found the universe's secret for accessing days that lasted longer than twenty-four hours. We were not that close, and yet we always had something to talk about. I had imagined we would become good friends, knitted together by the panic of deadlines, studying late into the inky nights. She'd once invited me to a mock UN General Assembly put on by social science and global studies students, most of whom she knew or knew of to varying degrees. I'd stayed in her shadow as she successfully navigated the social and political aspects of the meeting. She hurried around her large garden of flowers, taking a few sips of nectar from each. But I began to understand that I was not a significant flower in her garden, and I withdrew from my imaginings of being her close university friend and settled on being a friendly acquaintance.

I wondered if another might adopt me into their life. Other acquaintances were made here and there, and they became temporary friends for a term or two before they assimilated back into the masses. Small flickers of recognition and friendly glowing smiles briefly lit the long hallways on campus. This did not bother me. On the contrary, I had never seen the need to form close relations with more than two or three people. But having a Roslin was a must—that was non-negotiable—and I had one, and I was content. I had my Roslin. And so, I was free to disengage from the chaos of university, keeping to myself, unless specifically called upon by others.

Occasionally, I was pulled into attending parties, the first of which became a muted memory that summed up year one in my mind. I existed in the periphery, nearer to the edge of the solar system of students where the gravitational pull was weakest. The party was in a large boxy house, built during the time of cat-eye glasses, mint green, and Jell-O moulds. Miyu floated my way again with a drink I didn't ask for and gingerly placed the cup in my hands.

"Oh, it's alright if you don't know many people yet. You just get to know people, whether you like it or not." She laughed, and I smiled and took a sip of the drink because I had no response. The drink seemed to have conflicting alcohols in it: dry and fruity, sharp and spicy.

Miyu slipped through my fingers again and was in the center of another faction of individuals.

I was a singular statue between swirls of people who seemed liquid and easy. There was only one thing to do, and this was to take many tiny sips of the drink that had been placed in my hand.

I people-watched. There were girls on the arms of baby-faced boys, someone with every button of their collared shirt done up, girls with dewy makeup looking better than celebrities. A boy who towered over the room like a periscope. A post-mortem-thin body on the couch, deep-set hollow jade eyes. Boys trying to be men. Girls huddled in tight groups like football players. A grocery store-bought fruit tray with a peeling expiration sticker, and empty bowls with salted unpopped popcorn kernels left behind.

I dawdled away another forty-five minutes, while only exchanging a few smiles and faint nods with girls with flushed, friendly faces, who moved around me like a current.

When I decided that I simply could no longer pretend to be even remotely engaged in the party, I looked for the head of black hair that was unique to Miyu.

I tried to squirm through holes in the fabric of bodies, sometimes getting to where I wanted to go, sometimes finding myself ten steps behind where I had just been. When I saw someone I had a class with, I would freeze behind a larger body than mine or—*Aha!* I had caught her. The accomplishment of someone who had stood in a stream and caught a fish with their bare hands flickered through me.

Miyu's face radiated with the heat of human contact, vodka, and pizza. Her eyeliner was so delicate and perfectly aligned that it looked like God himself had stamped it on when she was a baby.

"I think I'm going to go now," I said loudly, yet my voice was drowned to a whisper in that house.

"Already? Okay, well, I'm glad you came out!" she said as she tucked her sleek black hair behind her ears, a perpetual habit.

We both leaned in for a short hug, a foot of air still between us, and then I departed.

A wave of happiness crashed over me as my hand finally grasped the handle of the front door and I passed to the other side of those four walls. Crisp air bit lightly. Maple tree leaves danced down the sidewalks. Moonlight glittered over rooftops, and everything was nearly beautiful except for shadows cast by the bending tree limbs that hung over the sidewalks. Tranquil evening menace.

The gentle warmth of a fuzzy brain—the result of watery vodka, cheap rosé, and something else that had made my mouth sour—lulled my restless thoughts. With no thoughts to contend with, I was a prisoner let out and uncuffed for a few brief moments of freedom. Pulling my sleepy feet over the pavement, one in front of the other, I soon came to a convenience store, all metal and dirty glass windows and ice cream advertisements. I wanted sugar. I wanted salt. Primal desires.

I placed gummy bears and kettle chips on the counter. The willowy cashier looked exhausted, but he managed to take my ten-dollar bill and make change.

I carried my treasure with one arm and held my phone with the other. Cold wind rippled my hair behind me as I kept on walking, more or less in a straight line.

A large cemetery stretched across the width of two city blocks, a black iron gate circling its entire perimeter. Crossing through the manicured lawn fraught with dead bodies would get me home much sooner, and I entered the cemetery at the next little gateway. In a different frame of mind, an evening walk through the graveyard may have been unnerving, but fear was not particularly present. Some headstones were new and spotless—recent deaths, a current mourning. Other headstones were much smaller and eaten away by the elements; whoever lay below had been dead so long. I had thought about joining them for years now—the ones below the earth. I had made this known to some therapists, and for others, I sealed those thoughts away from them. Rows and rows of different deaths laid in the earth, the deceased having walked through graveyards themselves gazing at those who had died before them.

I made it to the other side of the cemetery and would be back home in my apartment soon. It was one of the only parties I had gone to, and it felt like a mandatory student experience I did not want.

The Monday evening class ran late, and I did not get home to my apartment until after ten. Victoria was sitting in the window waiting, her small moon face and long whiskers silhouetted by the street light. I fed her and ate handfuls of blueberries. She quietly crunched on the kibbles. I leaned against the kitchen counter and let my eyes un-focus, turning everything in my apartment into a phantom mirage. My thoughts were untethered for several minutes until Victoria bumped into my leg, arching her back.

I turned off all the lights in the apartment except the warming glow of the bedside lamp. I sank into my bed fully clothed, and sleep pulled me into its dark waters.

A distant sound, constant in its intervals and noise, woke me. My limbs reached out toward the nightstand, and I said hello into the little rectangle to make the noise stop.

There was only the sound of popping sparks from a campfire on the other side of the phone, then several voices, and then finally Jesse's voice. It was three in the morning in my time zone, and Jesse was high again.

I pulled my blankets up to my chin and laid down on my side, letting the phone rest on the pillow beside me. I closed my eyes and listened as Jesse slowly strung sentences together. Happy Jesse, philosophical Jesse, confused Jesse, reminiscent Jesse. His moods varied during these kinds of phone calls. A boundary line would dissolve for Jesse, and he would be fluid and organic in his words, candid in a comforting way, like milk and honey. His voice was an extra blanket wrapping around me, and in that listless state, I felt that half my spirit was floating in the woods where he was.

I saw Jesse's soul as black and gold. I collected the gold bits and stored them in my mind, but Jesse had cut off circulation to parts of himself, and eventually, they died and fell away—those were the black bits.

Jesse's babbling, the pop and crack of campfire sparks, the sound of wind from four thousand kilometers away all culminated into a warm comfort that nestled around my tired body.

"I am calling for a reason," Jesse said after a while.

"And what's that?" I asked sleepily.

"I'm coming home soon. For a few days."

My eyes opened, and I picked up the cell phone to hold it several inches from my face. "You have a ticket booked?"

"It's booked."

A smile flashed across my face in the ink-black room. Excitement seeped into my tired body and ran steadily through my veins. The soap dispenser in the bathroom must be full the day he landed. A clean tea towel should be hung on the stove's door handle. The pictures hanging on the walls must be straightened. There could be no funny smells in the house. Cinnamon candles should be burned before Jesse stepped foot in the apartment. I needed to book a hair appointment for the upcoming weekend, just a trim, no dead ends.

It was only a few hours before I needed to be up, and I told Jesse I needed to sleep.

I ended the call, and exhaustion and excitement ricocheted through my body. I continued to make mental lists of tasks that needed to be completed before Jesse came home until sleep overtook me again.

II

First appointments were rarely extraordinary. The same script was more or less followed, and I had my lines more or less memorized. There was an art to therapy—sharing intimate details, pretending to ponder, throwing around red herrings to distract from things I couldn't talk about. Psychiatrists and counsellors might have differing ideas about what made up calming decor, but first appointments were the same.

Second appointments were for discovering the kind of person who sat across from you. Sonya knew her art well and asked questions that sliced through my stories, but she did it with the sweetest smile on her face. She knew what my previous diagnoses were, and she thrust the proverbial knife deeper every time I gave her a dismissive answer that only grazed the surface of the truth. The small shoulders pushed back against the white leather throne, the head bent to the left, just so, nearly imperceptible, the ears perceived mild deceit from my mouth. The woman, cunning yet never harmful, carried the paradox in her bones well. Gentle Machiavellian.

"Last week you shared that you have been diagnosed with OCD," said Sonya. "Tell me more about that."

There was silence as my thoughts scattered like cockroaches, the light too bright and pointed. It was near impossible to explain the constant and changeless things. Describe the colour green.

What, the merging of blue and yellow? Describe blue then. Describe yellow. Describe OCD. With what words?

"What would you like to know?" I asked.

"Well, you could start by telling me how OCD affects you." Silence still.

"Or you could explain how OCD manifests itself in your life."

"It's not the normal kind," I said. "Or the common one, I guess."

Sonya returned the favour of silence.

"Yes, I need some things to be a certain way, and I wash my hands an inordinate number of times, but that's only incidental for me. It's more in my head. I mean—" I threaded my fingers through the saffron fringe of a pillow. "—well, that's ridiculous, it's all in the head. I mean, my thoughts are intense, overwhelming, and hard to cope with. They get stuck in loops. It's like being locked in a room for weeks. That's how it feels. I have to organize the thoughts and deal with the fear that coats every thought, even the happy ones. It's like … a weird assembly line. Each thought comes along, there's an anxiety attached to the thought, then you have to figure out if it's a rational fear or not, then you go to the next fear-thought, and on and on. It takes so much time and energy just to think. Sometimes I would rather sleep and be unconscious than have to think."

Sonya looked solemn. "That sounds very tiring. I am sorry you deal with this." There was genuine care in her voice, in her eyes, in the way she clicked off her pen and listened closely. "Do you have positive thoughts, Imogen?"

"Yes," I replied. "Sometimes."

"Do those thoughts get played on a loop in your mind?"

"No. The positive ones are fine; I don't overthink those ones. There's no need."

"And you feel a need to think further on negative thoughts?"

"Yes."

"Why's that?"

"They're upsetting, and I have to figure them out."

The wind picked up, and through the windows the bare tree limbs swayed in the gusts and trembled in the lull between the sky's breaths.

"Can you tell me more about that?" Sonya asked. "What is the nature of these thoughts that are upsetting?"

I stayed silent, the wind did not. Forest raised her head from the cradle of her two paws and listened as the wind shrieked. The specifics of my OCD thoughts were a difficult part of my cocktail of mental illnesses to describe. It was the olive in the martini that I often picked out and threw away before offering it to my therapist.

"Maybe we could get into that another time when you are comfortable talking about it," Sonya said.

I had only ever told a few therapists in the past about the moralistic aspect of my mental illness, and every time I had disclosed this most personal piece of information, there was a sharp sense of embarrassment. Being amongst friends always caused me to stare at everyone and think that surely none of those people spent so much time in the convoluted mess of thoughts that I did. Yet there I would sit, sipping a weak mimosa, people all around me, secretly estranged and alienated from their reality. As if I had been placed on a slightly different trajectory than everyone else my age, our paths only crossing briefly at times when we were together, but then soon I would leave their orbit and be back in my own infernal world.

But this particular counsellor—Sonya—was neither fazed nor unresponsive to the oddities and depressing truths I spoke.

I opened my mouth, and it moved as if to form words, but no noise came out. Sonya waited. "When I was little," I said slowly, "I felt very close to *being bad*. Meaning, if I did a few things wrong, I would be considered *bad*. In elementary school, there was this huge field behind the school. Part of it was a gravel track, and at the far end of the field were trees. We weren't allowed to go to the far end of the field or be behind the trees because the teachers couldn't see us if we were there. So, of course, everyone wanted to go to the far end of the field and be behind the trees. But I didn't. I dreaded their little fits of rebellion. My friends would slowly drift further and further down the field, so that the teachers didn't notice, and I would inch along, hoping they would stop. They usually didn't, and I would get more and more anxious the closer we got to the place we weren't supposed to be." The memory was clear and crisp in my mind. "And I was terrified of the possibility of a teacher being mad at me. I obsessively worried about whether I was bad or not—I was too young for those kinds of thoughts."

I had been such an easy child to raise. Terrified of making others upset, operating with the maturity of a disciplined adult. Of course, the easy child became a complexly mentally ill teenager. And I felt alone, divided out, different from my peers.

Yet I knew I wasn't alone. There were many others walking through their own dark corridors, carrying their own burdens, thinking the exact same thoughts I was thinking, enclosed within their own four walls. I thought then that many people must be walking around with an arrow pierced halfway through their heart; some bleed internally, quiet bleating lambs, while others bleed out everywhere, coating everything they touched in deep crimson.

"Did those around you put a strong emphasis on *being good* when you were a child?" asked Sonya. "Your parents maybe?"

"Yes, they did," I replied slowly. "But—I mean, they didn't yell or get mad if I did something wrong. That's not who they are at all. I think I just knew there was a high standard of *good* I needed to be."

"Highly sensitive children can internalize those kinds of unspoken systems in their family."

I had soaked up everything—every stress and anxiety in the home had stuck to me and then morphed into me, until fear became the commodity of living.

The therapy session was winding down, and Sonya asked if I wanted to book our next appointment. I half-heartedly took the business card she elegantly held out to me between two fingers, a date and time written down on the back.

The atmosphere of the warm office gently dissipated as I walked to my car. A wild rabbit scampered across Sonya's driveway and dove into one of the bushes. *You don't have to run away from me*, I thought. But the dogwood stayed still and kept its fugitive safe.

The drive from Sonya's house on the outskirts of the city to campus was long. Patches of crocuses grew in front yards, their beautiful blue-violet colour stark against the dullness that was the complicated event of springtime. Receding banks of snow still clung to the curbsides, though the strengthening sunshine was changing the snow into water, and the water ran down the roads and into the sewers. Spring was overtaking winter and it was beautiful, refreshing, dismal, dreary; a season that encompassed new birth and bleak living.

Winter always held on for a long time like a friend overstaying their welcome at a house party. Winter never wanted the party to end, but either April or May would come and push it out. Time was always slipping away; it was a slow trickle that I could never successfully contain in my cupped hands.

I parked my car near the edge of a sprawling parking lot, one of the tentacles of the large campus that grew ever outwards. Thirty-some thousand students infested the campus, everywhere people walking, everywhere blue-white screens radiating off fatigued faces.

Sideline activities of leisure and interest were slowly set aside; time was divided and allotted between five courses, the remaining hours only allowing for activities that required not an ounce of energy—sleeping or gazing at a screen with moving images.

In Oracle, Arizona, there lived a failed scientific project covering several acres of land. Its name was Biosphere 2. The glass and steel structure of Biosphere 2 was meant to create an enclosed ecosystem, self-sufficient and self-sustaining. It was to be a miniature Earth on Earth. The biosphere failed: the humans went hungry, oxygen levels fell, plants and animals died, the ecosystems became dangerously unbalanced.

I would think of Biosphere 2 from time to time, when life felt especially absurd and artificial, when it looked certain that no one knew how to care for the fragile organic bodies we resided

16

in. I was merely a little specimen of fauna in an artificial kind of living, unsustainable and wildly unbalanced. A small but unrelenting disdain for modern society had been planted in my heart from a young age. Who or what planted the seed was unclear. I simply did not take to this life very well.

The world was sharp, stilted, heavily-monitored, unnatural, and stifling. The human spirit was organic, free-flowing, primitive, ineffable, and animate. A chasm formed, too wide for me not to notice as a child. I loved the latter and despised the former.

The world did not seem to be my home, neither as a child nor an adult. And so, I escaped. Small and frequent escapes. There were little hideaways throughout the campus body—oddly shaped nooks where old met new, brick met steel, the architects bled dry of ideas. I found them and hid, toting many memoirs along with me to those quiet places. I saw the little hells the authors hid between the printed lines. The worst of times could not be put into words anyway.

Final exams and papers were all slated for April. My time visiting Jesse would need to be carefully planned. I marked off each day's white square on the hanging calendar, giddy to soon be in Jesse's arms again. The wall calendar had been a Christmas present from one of Jesse's cousins, who studied communications in New York and was attached to the family by a thread. The cousin had gotten my name for the gift exchange. Pictures of kittens in watering cans, kittens with butterflies on their noses, and kittens in a teacup were printed on thin, flimsy paper. I suppose the cousin knew I had a cat. Still, I hung the calendar, as unsightly as it was, and harboured sentimentality toward it since it was from the first Christmas party Jesse's family had invited me to. The cement was setting in our relationship. Now all of Jesse's family knew that Jesse had a girlfriend, and that girlfriend was me, and the gaudy calendar was the wax seal of approval.

"Jesse," I said in a low voice. "Can you hear me?" I was on a phone call turned video call after Jesse insisted that the camera be turned on. Every piece of technology that could be pointed at me to replicate my image, I hated. I did not like the human body in the least. I was a spirit that had gotten locked in a human body that could be looked at. Some medieval curse. If my parents allowed it, I would destroy every picture of myself that existed.

I looked down and cupped my hand around the phone's screen, the bright sunshine making it difficult to see. It was morning for me and even earlier for Jesse. He was still in bed, rolled over on his stomach, fist propping up his chin. His coppery hair was getting longer with every passing week. I liked it. I told him that he should let nature have its way a little longer and see what happened, but he didn't like how the hair got in his eyes and dripped with sweat while he worked.

Seeing Jesse made me miss him. Being with Jesse made me feel more normal. I could listen to him talk about mundane things, ridiculous things, and latch on to his world, exiting my own for a time. I could briefly feel convinced of calmness in the shadow of Jesse's unconcerned demeanour when we were choosing between brands of mustard, simultaneously cursing someone under our breath, kissing goodnight.

The illusion of calm was sometimes calming in and of itself.

"You look very pretty today," Jesse said as I weaved through crowds of students.

I cast a smile downward. "Thank you. Now focus."

"I am focused." He was mostly only seeing my breasts and neck and the delicate gold chain necklace he had given me.

"Focus on the conversation. You will be landing at Pearson on Monday evening, right?" Jesse had always had difficulty operating within the space-time continuum, but I tried to make plans nonetheless.

"Yes."

"And your sister is picking you up?"

"She is."

"And you're remembering that in case that plan falls through, I am not able to come and get you because I will be in class at that time?"

"Yes, ma'am. I am on my own."

"You are." I shifted the phone to my other hand. "How are you, by the way?"

I paused and imagined the vast expanse between the two of us: all the deep forests, the bottomless lakes, and the melting snow.

"It feels like a long time," I said.

"Since when?"

"Since I last saw you. Since I kissed you last."

"Don't you go sentimental on me, kid. I will be there next week."

"I know," I said softly. The mass of bodies thinned, and there was less noise to take cover under. Jesse shifted positions on his bed. The morning light I had woken up to several hours earlier was just now seeping through the window beyond his shoulder.

I took a long look at the little box of Jesse on my phone. "I need to go, but I will see you soon."

Jesse rolled onto his back and held the phone high over his head, early morning light gentle like a halo around him.

"Okay," said Jesse. "I love you."

"I love you too."

"And I will see you next week."

"See you next week."

I ended the phone call with some trouble since my fingers were frozen from the wind's icy breath. Images of the undone dishes and the messy countertop back home grew and clouded my head. No peace could be had until they were looked after. I should have at least washed the dishes before I left that morning so that I only needed to dry them and put them away when I got home. I bit my tongue and dug my fingernails into my forearm to reset and force my mind to get off the merry-go-round.

"I'm home, Victoria," I called out softly upon entering my apartment later that day after classes. I listened for signs of life, but there was only hollow silence.

The apartment was untidy, and I felt like Sisyphus, constantly trying to make my home look and feel the way I wanted but without the time or energy. I tried cleaning for a while until I was too tired.

I found Victoria fast asleep, curled up tightly like a snail. I quietly sat down beside her and picked up the book I was reading, straining to tap into the frequency of the author's voice before the inevitable. The obsessive thoughts would awake, entangle my thoughts, and I would be pulled out of the story. There were worrying thoughts, a vacuum of time—both too much and far too little—would surface. There were mundane fears and extreme fears. Any anxiety would capture my mind and lock me up. A lurking monster and me, unsafe in my own head. I read until I could no longer, sighed, and placed the book back on the coffee table.

It was the first Monday of April. I was tracking Jesse's flight in my mind that afternoon. He would be flying from Vancouver to Toronto, the plane's path dipping slightly in a convex curve, flying over Montana, North Dakota, Minnesota, Wisconsin, and Michigan before entering Canadian air again.

I sat down at the back of the lecture hall and tapped my fingers on the fake wood tabletop. Right then, Jesse would be suspended thousands of feet above North Dakota.

And while I was heading to my last class of the day, Jesse was over Michigan.

I wandered around my apartment that evening, glassy-eyed and buried in my thoughts, watering succulents here, rearranging coffee table items there. I needed to know that he had landed safely and that Emily had, in fact, arrived at Pearson airport at the right time, at the right gate, and that she and Jesse had completed this logistical task.

A text at 8:47pm: *Landed. Driving home now.*

The tightness in my shoulders slowly relaxed. I was glad he was safe. Jesse would be picking me up in a few days on Friday evening. We would be driving the desolate backroads home, free of the city and washed up into a different world of calm.

I washed my face and climbed into bed like a tired sloth, slowly stretching legs and feet into the cool depths of the sheets.

But sleep refused me, adrenaline still left in my body. And so, I got up to deadhead all the flowering plants in the house. Finally, the floodgates of exhaustion broke.

I skipped the one class I had on Tuesday and cleaned. I vacuumed Victoria's cat hair away, dusted every surface, and did the laundry. It was a cleansing ritual. That's what tidying and cleaning was. Like going to church and coming back renewed.

I filled the kitchen sink with hot, soapy water and scrubbed in feverish concentration. The husky growl of an engine pulled me out of my reverie. And then I raised my head and looked through curtained windows to see his dusty black truck pull into my driveway. I blinked in case it was a nightmare. My apartment was my safe haven, and this was a breach. My heart rate quickened, and I frantically shut off the running water, letting the little China dish I was washing clatter into the sink, and turned off all the lights with soapy hands.

I sat down behind the couch and cradled my knees against my chest as the truck door slammed shut. My cheeks burned. He was not supposed to be there until *Friday*.

Jesse knocked on the door and I didn't move. Victoria softly padded along the floor and hopped up onto the window sill in curiosity. There was the faint sound of Jesse's muffled voice speaking to Victoria through the front window. He tapped on the glass and I let my head fall on my knees, feeling like a six-year-old, stupid and infantile.

My personal space was not to be intruded on. There was an invisible fortress that encircled my time, my thoughts, my home. Anyone who stepped across the line uninvited was registered as a threat.

Jesse knocked again, then came the loud buzz of my phone vibrating on the wooden coffee table. I didn't budge, and the buzzing stopped. There was an eerie silence before the buzzing resumed.

I knew I could crawl to the coffee table and get my phone without Jesse being able to see me through the window. Incoming call from *Jesse Rudkovskaya*. I bit my lip and accepted the call.

"Hello?" I said quietly.

"Hey kid, where are you?"

"I'm … out. Why?"

It was disconcerting to see Jesse through the window curtains as I heard his voice in my ear.

"Well, your car is here."

"Is where?" I asked innocently, as Jesse leaned against the porch railing.

"I'm here to visit you, baby," Jesse's voice lilted. "I'm at your front door. Are you going to be home soon? Or should I meet you somewhere in the city?"

I slumped down even further until I was half sprawled on the floor like a ragdoll. The paralysing grip of fear kept coming in waves, blacking out my vision. Trapped bird, bat in sunlight, tiger in a cage. Insane and idiotic. I tried to split away from myself and put my consciousness way up on the moon.

Sit on the moon, look at your situation on Earth. What do I choose to do when I detach myself from the fear?

Horrifically ignorant people thought that we, the mentally ill and considerably incapacitated, were unaware of how our illnesses looked to others.

"Jesse. You were supposed to be here on Friday, *not* today. We didn't plan this."

"If we had planned it, then it wouldn't be a surprise."

Did he truly not know? Was he such an inattentive boyfriend, or was I such a poor communicator?

"I really don't do well with surprises. They give me a lot of anxiety. I'm sorry if I didn't make that clear before."

"Okay, but I'm here now," Jesse said. My heart seized at the sharp edge of annoyance that trickled into his voice. "So where are you?"

"Jesse," I said. "I can't handle this. I cannot handle surprise visits. You know I have a lot of anxiety issues, and this is just so—" I covered the receiver with two fingers and exhaled shakily "—not good."

Jesse was no longer leaning against the porch railing in a lackadaisical manner. "I drove all the way here."

"I know."

"And you don't want to see me?"

"It's not that I don't want to see you. It's that this situation is very stressful for me."

He sighed. "So, I can't just wait here until you get home and at least say hi?"

I had mentally zoned out for a moment in a wave of anxiety. Fuck it. "Jesse, I am here, at home in my apartment."

"What?"

"I'm in my apartment and I'm about to have a panic attack. Please go home. I'm sorry, but please just understand that I can't handle this. I don't feel well." Jesse cupped his hands around his face and looked through the window, though I knew he couldn't see me. "Please just go home."

"Imogen, this is so stupid."

I knew that. The more he pushed, the more like a lunatic I felt.

"I truly feel bad and I'm sorry, but please just understand that I can't do stuff like this." I didn't particularly feel like crying, yet tears formed and slid down my face.

Jesse and I went back and forth on the phone for another ten minutes. He knocked on the door, I pulled my knees closer to my chest like a scared child. I told Jesse I was ending the phone call, it felt safer to text.

Please go home, I texted. *I'm sorry.*

This shouldn't be a big deal, Jesse replied.

Obviously, I know that. Remember me telling you about when my mom threw me a surprise party for my eleventh birthday and I had a really bad panic attack? This is just like that.

Jesse didn't respond immediately. Then there was the sound of his truck door shutting. *Okay. I'll see you on Friday.* An engine started and the thunder of the truck grew distant and then dissipated into silence.

I imagined this would be yet another quirk of having a slightly hysterical girlfriend that he could add to the list. Jesse did have a certain amount of grace for my anxieties and general nervous disposition; however, there was always a blankness in his eyes, a lack of depth. He couldn't quite grasp who I was, couldn't quite fathom my psyche. But he usually tolerated it.

I looked down at my hands. They were shaking as I stood up, and it took a moment to steady myself. Pulling open the doors of my closet, I peered into the dwindling supply of little smoky green buds that were stashed away in a plastic bag. I would need to contact Michelle soon and dish out another fistful of cash. Sinking down onto the couch, I rolled a joint and sealed it. After five minutes of hunting around my apartment for the lighter I always misplaced, I flicked alive a small, warm flame. Tiny embers burned at the end of the joint, and I opened my bedroom window, ushering the smoke out through the screen. Cold air pressed against my face, but my skin was hot and it felt good.

My own sensitivity stirred up small fires of burning anger against myself. I feared others harboured their own secret fires of anger against my sensitivity as well.

I went to the kitchen sink and picked up the little China dish I had been washing. It was beautiful, ornate with intertwined lavender and honeysuckle and gold trim—a fifty-cent second hand find—now chipped from the fall. It would work well as an ashtray, and I tapped off bits of dusty ash.

Once again, I pressed my face against the cold breeze that strained through the open window. The breeze made the dying embers dance in the ashtray. I tried not to think about the frustrated Jesse I had just sent away, cussing me out in his head. Instead, I blew smoke out through my nose like a dragon and focused on something immediately near me that demanded attention from the five senses—a standard cognitive behavioural therapy method.

There was a black outside world, a breeze pushing around me and into the apartment, rustling leaves from last fall dancing past the window, the smell of a ripening earth, the taste of marijuana in my mouth.

The days were now stretching out, demanding the sun tarry in the blue, glassy sky just a while longer. That evening the light dimmed slowly. The sun would stay out later and later as the weeks slipped by and would end the days in brilliant ombre skies.

The southern edges of Canada saw a wide array of weather, went through every stage of grief, recognized each equinox. It was a small wonder to have been brought into the world on a tract of earth cradled between five Great Lakes, equal measures of wilderness and city lights.

I blew the last cloud of smoke through the window before shutting it. The phone remained untouched for the rest of the night; I didn't want to explain the shame already coating my lungs like a black tar.

III

On Thursday morning Miyu reached out to me once again, this time with an invitation to study with her and some others.

Although we did not communicate regularly, she seemed to remember to pass along invitations to me, and I found this to be unexpectedly kind.

"Who are the others?" I asked.

I wanted to know what her short list looked like. Since Miyu knew everyone, the possibilities were endless.

Miyu listed a few names that I had seen on our class list and said to meet at a certain cafe at four in the afternoon.

Everything was already packed and ready for Friday when Jesse would be coming back to the city to pick me up. And so, against my instincts, I decided to socialize. I brushed my hair out and pulled it into a neat, tight ponytail. Then I coated my eyelashes in black mascara muck before putting myself together with some semblance of fashion.

The cafe was warm, and the rich scent of espresso would never come out of the old wooden floorboards and would always cling to the high-vaulted ceiling.

"Americano, no room," I said and smiled at the barista.

There was one long table near the back of the cafe where we could sit and study.

By four-thirty, I was still the only one to have reached the meeting place. By five, I ordered herbal tea so that my heart would not burst from caffeine. A woman with dull grey eyes sat down on the chair to my left, which was entirely unnecessary since there were several other options.

A text message from Miyu: *Change of plans! Sorry. Studying at Miriam's.*

I felt like going home, but I asked for Miriam's address. Miyu already knew I was available to study and because Miriam did not live far from the cafe, I felt obligated to go. I drank the rest of the lemon chamomile and wearily packed up my things.

Miriam's was a small square home, a product of the 60s, with godawful awnings hanging over the windows and front door, looming vinyl to ward off sunlight and maintain dour living. I knocked and Miyu answered; I pulled my face into a smile. Bubbling over and drawing from her bottomless well of energy, Miyu introduced me to Hannah, Salomé, and the hostess, Miriam. Instead of a table and chairs, the girls were seated on pastel floor cushions circling a coffee table. It was intimate and endearing. I folded my legs and sat between Miyu and Salomé. Salomé sat with excellent posture, poised like a ballerina, and I immediately imitated her. Textbooks and laptops were scattered around, but studying was not happening. Salomé had a quick wit and a vivacious energy, sweet and enthralling. Beside her I felt dull and listless. I often felt like broken glass amongst a sea of girls who were alluring gems—cobalt blue sapphire, blushing ruby, plum amethyst.

While the outside of the house looked worn, the inside held dynamic energy. An entire wall had polaroids taped all over it— faces with the unnatural glow of a camera flash, sparklers and flaming campfires, graduation gowns, and house party poses. Whenever the conversation around the coffee table waned, my eyes wandered back to the wall of polaroids. I was fascinated with the lives they led, the normalcy, the predictability.

Mismatched wine glasses and blood-black merlot adorned Miriam's hands after one of her trips to the kitchen. A sum total of zero studying had been done. Five glasses of wine were poured, the bottle bled dry.

"I should have gone to sommelier school," said Hannah, swirling the wine into a whirlpool. "That would be an enjoyable school, I think."

"But you would be sitting in class with the personalities of people who want to be sommeliers," said Miyu.

"And I would drink to forget they were there," Hannah said, shrugging delicate shoulders.

I took a sip from the glass placed in my hand and once again remembered why I favoured white wine.

The girls started talking about some of the boys they studied with. Miriam had taken an interest in one of the university's hockey league players—Justin. Miyu had gone to high school with him.

"Look, I know your ex," said Miyu to Miriam. "And I know Justin. Justin is a nice boy, but you would be descending from Isaiah's level of intelligence to Justin's. So, mind the gap."

Miriam pretended to punch Miyu's arm as she laughed and sputtered on the wine she was drinking.

I had hardly spoken since I had arrived and was more of a ghost than anything. The girls talked over, around, and through me, and I was grateful, yet mildly put off. When one of the four girls had forgotten I was there, I would gently study them, in curiosity and admiration. Curved profiles, white teeth, earrings shimmering in the light. What were they like, what did they eat, who were they when they were alone? I imagined unzipping myself from my body and stepping into one of their skins. If I were in Salomé's body, I would have long, delicate fingers, with fingernails bitten down to nothing. Why did she bite them? And who was the initial N for on the tiny, gold pendant that hung from the bracelet on her wrist? Why did I wonder about these things?

Hannah had a dusting of freckles on her nose, cheeks, and arms. Her lips had taken on a pinkish stain from the red wine.

I looked at Miriam and wondered what sort of DNA had been perfectly mixed together to create the ethnically ambiguous beauty sitting on the other side of the coffee table. *God, could I be her?* Debilitating depression and anxiety surely must be marginally more bearable if you looked like a celestial being merely gracing the earth with your presence.

A happy dullness set in once I had emptied my glass. The sun was going down; Miriam turned on a couple of lamps. I was ready to go home.

The following day the sun forgot to shine as the slate sky suffocated in stratus clouds. And yet there was always a lightness to a Friday morning; expectations were about to subside for the next two days. There would be time to make a good breakfast— banana pancakes, cubed honeydew—and time to distinguish between the different bird songs that fell from tree branches.

I finished gathering up everything needed for a weekend away and paced around the apartment aimlessly, waiting for Jesse. The surprise visit fiasco had turned to dust and blown away. Neither Jesse nor I had mentioned it since.

My phone screen glowed with Jesse's text: *Five minutes away.*

I tricked Victoria into the cat carrier. Her eyes turned into giant black saucers inside two tiny rings of olive green.

Jittery euphoria made my hands shake. Waiting, waiting, until he was there, the truck door opening, his leg stepping onto the pavement. Worn blue jeans with steady footsteps. I opened the front door. My gaze was always drawn to his arms since they looked like home to me and I catapulted out of the house.

Jesse bent down slightly, waiting to catch my much smaller frame in his embrace. I twined my arms around his back and his warm mouth opened to kiss me.

"You made it," I said.

"I did," Jesse replied.

"You're home."

"Yes."

He kissed my neck, and I held him tightly for a moment before packing my things into the truck. Jesse arched an eyebrow in good-humoured dismay at the unreasonable amount of luggage I carted around for a weekend away.

An hour of driving felt like mere minutes, and soon the fields and stretches of woods were beginning to look familiar, like old acquaintances. I would gently tap on the cat carrier to keep Victoria's attention on me and less on the terrifying world. Budding trees lined the country roads, patiently waiting for warmer temperatures before they unfurled. The crabapple trees around Jesse's home would blossom into fuchsia pink, and then the tiny crimson crabapples would ripen and fall to the ground, left to rot.

A tree that Jesse had carved our names into passed by. The tree was a tall and proud red maple, and I had been about to tell Jesse not to hurt its bark, but he had already started carving and I didn't want just *Imogen* to be engraved on the tree—not when I was the only Imogen around those parts. And so there it was, slashed into the tree: *Imogen* + *Jesse,* with a misshapen heart encircling the two names.

We turned into Jesse's gravel driveway. The ageing yellow-brick Victorian house he had bought for a song stood quietly in overgrown shrubbery that was swallowing up the decrepit concrete slab front porch. The house was empty for most of the year, save for the handful of times that Jesse was home, and it was deteriorating too quickly. A silver wind chime sounded softly in the breeze; it had remained faithfully hanging at the front of the house since before Jesse had moved in. The wind chime was usually the solitary sign of movement.

"Should we leave my things in the truck?" I asked Jesse.

"You're not staying here tonight?" Jesse asked.

"Am I?"

"Aren't you?"

I never wanted to assume these things, and I, in turn, did not want Jesse to assume I would open my apartment door to him at any given time either. We each silently decided to not continue the conversation.

Jesse opened the side door to the house and held it for me.

The kitchen was somehow both a mess and barren. Bills, letters, and flyers piled up on the counter, succulents that miraculously stayed alive because of his mom's occasional watering lined up on one window sill, empty beer bottles lined the other. It was a bachelor's sty, but it felt good and stable to be back in that house—with him.

Jesse sidled up to me and kept kissing my arms and shoulders as I opened his fridge. The shelves were completely bare save for several bottles of condiments.

"You need to get food for the week," I said.

"I'll be eating at my mom's mostly," Jesse replied between kisses.

"Still." I spun to face him. "You need sustenance." I pulled Jesse to me and kissed him. Being around my boyfriend caused an interesting anomaly. A temporary firewall blocked out anxieties and I mimicked the way he held on only loosely to the reins of life.

We made it to his bed, clothes disappearing off our bodies and dropping to the dusty floor along the way. I twined my body around Jesse. He called me his koala bear sometimes. I liked feeling him against me, soft skin over hard muscle.

"You could be the statue of David," I had told him once. He had the sturdy body of someone moulded by the elements and sculpted by long days of manual labour.

"What's that?" The hot sun on Jesse's bare back had made it glimmer as he hauled flagstone to his backyard for a fire pit.

"Don't you know what the statue of David is?" I'd blinked against the glare of the gaseous fire ball. Jesse continued hauling stone.

"No, I don't," he replied.

Jesse's breath was hot in my ear and I closed my eyes and focused on the here and now. Sometimes my mind wandered even during sex, not because I was uninterested, but merely because my mind was a racehorse that never stopped.

Stay in your body this time.

I put my hand on the back of Jesse's warm neck and breathed in his scent—smoky outdoor air, linseed, and sweat.

I fell into a fitful sleep afterward, the cotton sheet tangled around my legs. The room had become uncomfortably warm. I dreamt that a small white candle had been lit and immediately left unattended. The candle sat on a wooden table that stood in the middle of a hollow white house. The house was one large square room with large square windows, a single staircase ascended to the second floor. I was vaguely familiar with the beautiful austerity of the room, and I sensed the upstairs was no different from the floor below it.

The heat of the candle flame made the white wax pool around the wick before it quickly spilled over into rivulets. And then, quite suddenly, I turned around and left the house through a large door that opened to fields of tall grass and honey-coloured wheat that stretched out forever into the horizon. The sea of grass and wheat resisted my presence, just as waist-high water resisted one's wading. Rolling fields, thick and never-ending, surrounded the white structure. I kept on walking in that eternal field, lost in it forever perhaps. Abruptly, I reached a clearing, far from where the house should be, and yet there the house was, just ahead of me, on fire, mountains of red-hot flames seething out of its windows. Heavy smoke billowed upward and blackened the once clear sky. The caving roof collapsed in despair, its last breath a firework display of ash and embers.

My body convulsed as I left the dream and woke into a haze of anxiety. The movement had disturbed Jesse; however, he did not wake up, he merely sighed in his sleep.

I gently rolled to the side and inched my way out from under the bedsheets. I glided my hand over the wooden railing top that lined the upstairs hallway and made my way to the bathroom. Quietly shutting the toilet seat's lid, I sat on top of it, pulling my legs and feet up from the floor. The day was ageing and the light that filtered through the frosted glass window was dim and muted. It was the weary end of winter that must occur before the birth of spring.

Jesse had been home in January, and that was when I'd seen him last. We had gone snowshoeing on a ribbon of a trail near his mother's house. The hike had been lovely; the sky was that shade of winter blue, and a weak wind shook the naked limbs of trees, occasionally causing bits of snow to fall off the branches and join the rest of their kin on the ground. I could never fully understand those who despised winter as Jesse's mother did. Of course, there were unpleasant days between the months of November and March, but nothing in any other season compared to the brilliance of a winter day when the sun hung high in the sky, its warmth only just reaching Earth, its light shining on the snow, making everything in its path shimmer. On those pristine days, the earth was diamond encrusted, crisp, and calm. That purity was not found in summer.

The hike had been a happy one, and I'd felt exhausted from fresh air and laughter. But all was overshadowed and forgotten when we emerged from the woods and into the clearing at the back of the property to see a sullied green pickup truck idling in the driveway. The truck belonged to Jesse's father. Jesse's mother, Linda, stood on the back porch, arms crossed and only covered with a thin white sweater, shivering.

"Shit," Jesse said quietly.

We both bent down to unstrap the snowshoes from our feet.

Byron's heart could not be found; it did not show up, even in the presence of his three children. Sometimes I wondered where it had been lost, or what it had been lost to.

Jesse told me once that Byron was a shining model.

"A what?" I had asked.

"A shining model of a defective father," Jesse said.

Byron lived in a log cabin among unruly bush and sappy trees. The cabin had been nice when he moved in after the divorce, but it had become increasingly decrepit as each year passed. Unpiled firewood and rusting metal tools littered his small yard. Byron left the property when he ran out of alcohol, needed cigarettes, or was stocking up on the canned goods and processed meats that were his sole sustenance.

"Shit, alright." Jesse picked up his snowshoes. "Let's go."

Being calm and collected in situations that did not involve me personally was not so very difficult, and so I followed suit and picked up my snowshoes, stepping in the indents Jesse's boots made in the snow.

Byron's relationship with Jesse rarely looked like a father-son relationship. The time they did spend together was often on bar stools when Byron didn't want to be alone to drink. Byron's call was a sickening one. It was a mouthful of dust, misleading as the sirens' call. Jesse almost always said yes when his father asked for company alongside his drink, and I think he hated himself for it. But if he did not take up his dad on those offers, there would have been no relationship to speak of.

Once, when I was picking Jesse up from a drafty box of a bar, Byron had asked me for my number. I said no and Jesse said no. It was unlikely that he remembered I was his son's girlfriend when his mind sloshed with beer.

We were only several yards away from the house when Linda looked up and nodded at us.

Byron, aware of her averted gaze, turned around. "Afternoon," he said.

"Afternoon," Jesse and I muttered in unison.

Linda pulled her thin sweater more tightly around herself. "Byron is leaving."

Byron's weathered face smiled in a way that revealed no pleasantness. "I was only here to pick up something of mine."

I looked at Linda to see if that was the truth, but her face was still and resolute.

Byron nodded at me to acknowledge my presence in this family circle. An awkward silence ensued, and Byron said he needed to be somewhere and made his way to the idling truck.

Linda turned her back once he was off the property and opened the door for us. "He wasn't here to pick anything up. He was here asking for money for another house project."

Another verse of the same song. Byron would think of something he needed to do to his log cabin and would ask family and friends for money, usually around the end of the month when the funds from the disability cheque ran dry. If he was lucky and someone did give him money, he would spend it on his favourite bottles of amber whiskey. Linda had initially given

Byron money from time to time and was nervous when his hydro was turned off after bills had gone unpaid, but she stopped the cash flow long ago.

When I first began spending time with Jesse's family, I had felt sheltered from the reality of a dysfunctional family. I came from a family where couples stayed married and children grew up in non-volatile environments. I had listened with utmost discomfort as Linda swore at her siblings over the phone. Linda was a tired woman who needed a reprieve. She tried to have patience with others but had a tongue of fire that was often fanned into flame. She was a smoker constantly trying to quit, and the edges of her second-hand designer purses were fraying.

Linda tried her best, but sometimes it just wasn't enough, and she could not have possibly been there for her children as often as they had needed her.

I had told Jesse to go to a counsellor once, and he shot the idea down in seconds. Counselling was only for the *very fucked up*, he had said. I didn't know if he remembered that I was in counselling.

Feeling more tired now than I had before sleeping, I washed my hands for no particular reason and padded back to the bedroom. I stopped short when I realized Jesse's eyes were open and that he had watched me come back into the room.

"Oh," I said. "Hi."

"Howdy," said Jesse.

I snuggled up beside his warm body and placed my hand on his arm. Silence ensued, and I thought maybe Jesse had fallen back asleep until I felt him stir again.

"Anna and Kieran are having a house party tomorrow night. They've invited us." Jesse yawned.

A silent sigh welled up within me, though I chose not to audibly release it. "And do we have to go?"

"We haven't seen them in a while. So I think so."

Anna and Kieran had started dating around the same time as Jesse and me, and because Kieran and Jesse had been friends since high school, it was expected that Anna and I would naturally form a friendship as well. We did bond, cautiously, like two children told to play together. Kieran had not been named Kieran at birth, but only his oldest friends could remember what his real name was.

Both Anna and Kieran were tall and lean-muscled, moderately more attractive than either Jesse or me, and I sometimes joked that they were Jesse and Imogen 2.0.

"You might be able to upgrade to an Anna someday," I had once said to Jesse.

"No thanks, kid," was his reply. It made me feel good.

I realized that I had been silent for a moment too long and Jesse must have taken it for disapproval, which I was in fact feeling but trying not to express.

Jesse ran his finger down the bridge of my nose. "I'm sorry, I only found out about the party this morning."

"Okay, alright," I said. "Tomorrow night you said?"

"Yes. We don't have to stay for the whole thing."

We fell back asleep, closely knit together under the covers. When I woke up the room was completely dark, without even the faintest light of the moon. We quietly descended the stairs as if the house itself was still asleep.

Jesse took out his phone and showed me some of his photos as we sat on the couch, curled into each other like a fiddlehead. He had taken pictures of towering trees, baby saplings, doe-eyed deer, pristine lakes. There were pictures of Jesse with his arms around friends, dirty with mud, faces aglow in both sunshine and campfire light. The lifestyle was untamed and rugged and it was where Jesse's heart could roam free. There was no dad, there was no mom; it was just Jesse. Even a few of his inner demons had been convinced to stay behind in Ontario.

Evening came, and I climbed out of Jesse's bed only to climb into my own as soon as I arrived at my parent's home. It was the same bedframe I had been climbing onto since I was nine years old.

I pulled the blankets up to my chin and tried to melt into a pleasant sleep. The images of grass, house, and fire flung themselves around in my mind, like a bird trapped in a building.

IV

The hours kept passing as I madly scrounged together a compilation of statistics and quotes that I could build into a scholarly-sounding paper. Thoughts of the party pushed their way to the forefront of my mind as the afternoon melted away.

I took a shower and chose a house party-worthy outfit for the evening. I did not tell my parents that I was going to a house party, only that I was going to the house of a friend.

My parents were a delicate glass plate that I needed to keep up in the air and never let fall to the ground. It was a vigilant acrobatic act I had been playing for years. They simply could not ever see every angle of myself, I had to distort the stage lighting just a little. It was still me they saw, me glowing in a certain angle of lighting, but it was not me in the harsh light of day.

Jesse's headlights shone into our large country windows, the blinding landing of a spaceship, and I slipped out of the house before he could come to the door. I maintained a small barrier between my boyfriend and my parents. The barrier was built of different things: short dinners at restaurants that ended when the food was finished and before the real talking could begin, a history of Jesse so polished that it reflected their own ideals, Christmas cards with lovely verses and Jesse's signature at the bottom. If the boyfriend and the parents mixed too closely there would be complications. Jesse would say something my parents didn't like or my parents would ask too many questions about Jesse's life and I would be the obligatory mediator.

The front porch light was warm and glowing when we arrived at Anna's.

Anna's parents owned a thriving landscaping company, and in our circles, they were upper echelon. Anna met us at the door, her naturally bleach-blonde hair hanging around her head like a halo of light. She belonged to that small population of humanity that need not try to be beautiful and yet beauty clung to them. Her cheekbones were angled just right, her hair was naturally salon-grade.

Kieran and Jesse were immediately subsumed into the living room of party guests. It was not a large party; there were only ten or twelve of us. I knew all of their names and backgrounds, and yet *friend* was not a word I could attach to many. I instinctively followed Anna, the girl I knew the best, into the kitchen where it was quieter. She began preparing snacks for the evening. I asked her how I could help and she told me I could set out the chips and salsa and guacamole.

"How are you and Jesse?" Anna asked as I spooned store-bought guacamole into a glass bowl.

"Oh, we're fine," I said. "It's been a couple of months since he was home last, so it's good to see him again. However, I am also trying to ensure I graduate next month. So my mind is on a few other things."

Anna nodded sympathetically. "Kieran always picks the worst times to visit me. He can't plan ahead."

"Neither can Jesse."

"It's cute though—" Anna poured herself a glass of wine. "—Kieran has surprised me with visits a few times since I moved to Toronto."

I kept dutifully spooning out salsa into another bowl, and said rather flatly, "That is cute." Images of Jesse's surprise visit flashed.

The conversation circled around mundane topics. I glanced at the kitchen clock and saw that only thirty-five minutes had passed. Time was a tricky optical illusion in the company of others when minutes felt like hours. Anna offered to top up my glass of white wine and I held it out for her to do so.

"What are you doing next year after you graduate?" I asked.

"I'm planning to go straight into law school," Anna said.

This was not surprising since Anna had a bottomless pit of motivation and was the kind of student that universities portrayed in their advertisement propaganda.

"Very cool," I said and took another sip of wine that left my breath smelling like old flowers. "Which law school do you want to go to?"

Anna leaned her body against the arm she had rested on the kitchen counter. She wore a tiny gold chain bracelet around her wrist—this adornment and nothing else. Not even her ears were pierced.

"Well," she said. "I'm not sure yet. Kieran doesn't want me to be far from here," she gestured vaguely at what I assumed to mean the county we lived in. "York was far enough for him. You know he hates Toronto. To him, it was like I was in the lion's den—a miracle I made it out. Let's go to the sunroom," Anna said abruptly.

I followed her into the sunroom that was never used outside of the summer season. It was frigid and I chose to sit down on the couch seat closest to the door, in hopes that warm air would slip through under the door.

Anna sat down opposite me and crossed her thin legs. "I've always wanted to be a lawyer, you know. That's who I am. But lately, Kieran has been acting as if my going to law school is brand new information to him. He didn't care that I wanted to go to law school a few years ago, but the closer I get to doing it, the more he acts like it's a personal affront." Anna drained her glass.

I looked at her. The kitchen light softly shone into the dark sunroom and illuminated her eyes and arms. She was a little human package of ambition and thought and speech and hazelnut eyes and favourite foods and playground memories.

"He said it would be easier on me—on us—if I was a legal secretary or something."

"Easier on you?" I asked. "What does that mean?"

"Well." Anna slowed her speech down to molasses, her way of methodically thinking through things before speaking. "For one, I don't think he wants us to be far apart, distance-wise. But ..." she slowed even more "... it also feels like he's worried about me being a *lawyer*. While he is a plumber."

"He's scared of that?" I asked. I knew Kieran well enough to know that he had an ego. Sometimes it was in check, sometimes it wasn't. Kieran did not like to be challenged and anything he couldn't comprehend he would write off as useless. The knowledge he had acquired by the age of eighteen had become his gold standard, nothing needed to exceed it. And Anna exceeded it.

"I don't know," said Anna. "I guess he probably feels threatened. It's just too much post-secondary for him maybe."

"Maybe he feels like you'll be out of his league," I said. "All the learnin' and lawyerin'."

Anna interrupted with a light laugh. "It's ridiculous sometimes. He has such an ego." She tapped her fingers on the armrest of the chair. "I think he should have lived a century ago. He would have felt like he had more ... authority. Or importance."

I moved my body slightly to the left so that I could catch the streak of moonbeam shining through the trees and into the sunroom on my lap. "Anyway," I said. "I don't know if you were asking for advice about Kieran or not. I hope not because I don't really have any. It's only you who can decide where your priorities lie."

Anna and Kieran had been dating for almost three years. But perhaps dating him had become more of a habit than a choice.

"I guess I feel that ending things with Kieran and moving on would almost be like confirming that I can't work in my field and he in his." Anna looked up to heaven. "Sometimes he tries to correct me when I talk about the legal system."

"Does he cite sources?" I bit my lip and smiled and Anna did too.

"Kieran doesn't read. What's he going to cite? A dream?"

I laughed and clicked my tongue. "The castle of self-importance that Kieran has built for himself in his mind is invisible to the rest of us, but god, you're his girlfriend. Why can't you just play pretend with him?"

A triangle of light appeared on the rug between Anna and me, growing larger as Jesse pushed open the sunroom door.

"What are you girls doing in here? There is a party."

"What are you doing out there that's so great?" Anna quipped.

"Having a good time. Want to join?" Jesse pushed the door open wider.

I stretched my legs. "We're coming."

As it turned out, the rest of the partygoers were not doing anything spectacular. Camille and Amanda were there—girls who I had occasionally hung out with during my short stay in a brick-and-mortar high school. I hadn't seen either of them for a long time. Camille had gone out east to Dalhousie; Amanda had gone out west to Simon Fraser. That was the thing about living in a country that stretched from sea to shining sea: after high school graduation, everyone can scatter to the four winds. Shiloh and David were there too. Shiloh had a tall girl by his side, likely his new muse.

Anna poured me another glass of wine, I thanked her and retreated to the least inhabited corner of the living room.

Ten o'clock, then eleven o'clock passed. Amanda and Shiloh and Shiloh's girl scurried out of the house at one point when they heard coyote cries. The door slammed too loudly as each of them went outside. The girls, like a herd of sheep, meandered to the rec room, following the first girl who had departed from the front room. The boys soon followed.

"What are you girls doing?" asked Mark.

"Seeing who can smile like Mona Lisa," said Anna as all the girls stood in front of a large mirror.

This is a strange party, I thought. We all knew each other from high school, but only a small number of us were actually friends who had remained in contact with one another. Mark brought out a deck of cards and explained a drinking game. I quietly sighed as I was dealt in. Jesse sat down beside me on the couch and I cocooned into his side. He looked down at me and I changed my face into a pleasant look, though I could feel my eyes stayed dull. Jesse didn't seem to notice.

The game was vulgar and foolish and I found my mind leaving my body and floating up and out of the window between each of my turns. Jesse became agitated when Kieran and David made stupidly high bets on the outcome of the card game.

"You have to have more grace for formula babies," I whispered in Jesse's ear and looked at my cards. "I kid," I said and smiled up at him.

I saw the thin gold chain necklace I had given Jesse for his birthday sparkle in the lamplight. I was enamoured by the individual gold chain links that made up the necklace for a full minute and then blinked, realizing I was drunk. I put my heavy head on Jesse's shoulder and let it rest there. After a few minutes, he shrugged the burden of my head off his shoulder, laughed, and told me to pay attention to the game.

My head was feeling heavy. A thick fleece lined my brain, rendering all stimuli to be simultaneously too much, yet not enough for me to be able to focus on any one thing. My thoughts were slow to surface, but I knew that I was ready to go home.

"Jesse," I murmured into his ear. "I feel like I'm going to fall asleep any second. Can we go home soon?"

"It's not even midnight yet, Mo," he replied. "Can you hang in there a little longer?"

"I'm exhausted, Jesse."

He sighed. "Alright, we'll leave in a bit."

Leaving *in a bit* meant nothing, of course. I opted out of the card game soon thereafter. My head kept naturally falling to the side and onto Jesse's shoulder as my arms and legs and chest softened. Time was passing more quickly outside of my head than inside of it. The buttery warm light of the kitchen shone into the room where we sat and made me blink. My gaze strayed to where the shadows lay. I could hear the dull laughter—some of it I perceived to be disingenuous—around the coffee table in front of me. I felt permeable and weakened, the darkness of the shadows suddenly much closer to me than they really were.

"Jesse," I whispered so softly that I knew he couldn't have heard it. "Jesse," I said again.

Jesse tilted his head slightly downwards toward me. "Yes?"

"I don't feel well."

"What?"

"I said I don't feel well."

"What's wrong?"

I felt anxiety building up pressure against the weak walls of the dam that kept panic attacks at bay. I grabbed Jesse's hand and held it in a vice.

"Mo, what is wrong?"

"I'm going to have a panic attack." Oddly I wanted to cry. I cried so rarely.

"Actually?"

"Yes, actually."

"Doesn't alcohol calm you down, though?"

I looked at him. "I am going to have a panic attack."

"Okay. I don't know what to do. What should I do?"

Jesse was aware that I had panic attacks. I never believed that he really comprehended how vicious they were or what death felt like in the form of fear and despair, but at least he knew of them.

"I need to get out of here. Or at least I need to go to a quiet place." I caught Anna looking at me funny, perplexed.

Jesse placed his hand of cards face down on his knee. "Do we have to leave?" He asked reluctantly.

My chest was contracting and my breath was shortening. The external world hardly existed, only a hell in my mind felt real.

"I can't be here on this couch right now." I tried to loosen my grip when I saw Jesse's fingers turning a pomegranate red in my own hand, white and bloodless. "I'm going to go to the bathroom. Please come." I pushed myself off the couch and ignored Anna's stare. Maybe others took notice too, but I wasn't aware of it.

I sat down in the bathroom with my back against the bathtub. Impending doom, fuzzy brain; it was hard to tell if the wine was softening the sharpest edges of panic or only making them sharper.

Jesse closed the bathroom door and leaned against it.

I dropped my forehead until it rested on my knee. My mouth silently formed the words of Emily Dickinson. "I felt a Funeral, in my Brain, And Mourners to and fro, Kept treading - treading - till it seemed, That Sense was breaking through."

"Mo," said Jesse.

I looked up. His eyebrows were sewing themselves together, whether in frustration or confusion, I did not know because I could not bring any particular thing into focus. "I don't know what to do right now. I don't really know what this is." He gestured to my general aura.

"It's a panic attack," I said.

"And how do you end them?"

"I don't. Or at least, I can't. They just end themselves after a little while."

"You scare me when you get like this."

"What?" I said. "I haven't had a panic attack in front of you before."

"No, I mean it's weird when you get anxious and panicked in general. You get this look in your eyes like you're not really there."

"Sorry to be weird then."

Jesse stooped down and sat on the bathroom floor himself. "I'm not criticizing you."

I already knew what Jesse meant. Of course I wasn't *there*, in the present, when I was fending off my own bad thoughts. I couldn't be in two places at once.

I asked Jesse to talk about anything else. Anything mundane, anything at all.

Jesse described his favourite forest in B.C. It sounded beautifully unworldly and I nodded numbly as he spoke. Thick bark, mossy rocks, wild ferns, many bears, precious freedom.

The panic passed as it always did. But even acknowledging that it would pass during the panic did nothing to soothe.

When we re-entered the living room, I became acutely aware of how drunk everyone was. Jesse had not appeared to be too intoxicated in the bathroom; he held his liquor quite well. I was stepping over several pairs of legs as I made my way back to our seats when I saw Anna and Kieran look past me, or maybe through me, and make a sliver of meaningful eye contact with Jesse. It was infantilizing, but I was used to it.

I had no idea if Jesse had told his friends much about my health. But truly I did not care one iota. I had stopped caring three or four years prior. Most of the time when people knew there was *something wrong* with me, they distanced themselves emotionally to a certain degree. Maybe they simply did not know how to deal with invisible health problems or perhaps they thought they should give me space to be crazy.

Give her space, she has issues, let her be.

I rarely liked to be around people. Quite honestly, I revelled in my neuroticism when it meant fewer people in my path.

The only flaw in this phenomenon was the infantilization that some people blended in with their concern for me. Sometimes it was interesting to observe them observing me, and it was comical until they doubted my cognitive ability.

But I thought, devastatingly too much. I considered mortality and immortality, parallel universes, photosynthesis, the existence of a nonphysical spirit outside the physical body, anarchy, life as a fawn in a forest. Bones and muscle could enclose so many immaterial thoughts and emotions.

The following hour was warped and blurry like old glass—sixty minutes subsequently pushing each other out of the way. The panic attack had passed and Jesse rubbed my back from time to time as I sat beside him in a crumpled mess.

I became like the sun and no one could make direct eye contact. They were uncomfortable. So they did know something.

Anna hugged me goodbye sometime long after midnight and whispered a soft, "Are you okay?" in my ear. I nodded, smiled, and said I was fine.

The drive home in Jesse's truck was not long, but my heavy head leaned against the passenger window and my eyes closed.

Between Jesse's truck and his house was snow-wet grass and flagstone, swirling and slowly churning like upset waters before my feet. A bad hangover would be waiting to greet me the next morning.

Although I had a toothbrush at Jesse's, I skipped the ritual that night. Unthinkable under normal circumstances. I was in bed before Jesse, and I curled up on the left side of the bed, pulling the soft cotton blankets up to my chin. Then, remembering the little blue sleeping pills beside me, I propped myself up on my elbow and slid the top drawer of the oak nightstand open to reveal the little plastic bag I kept them in. I never had a good sleep without them. Everything looked doubled and tripled, moving and turbulent, churning waters smashing into the rocks, ocean spray fireworks. I had not remembered to bring water to the bedside. No water, but no matter; I sleepily collapsed back onto my pillow and the little blue pill made its way down my esophagus somehow.

A slight jolt to the bed—Jesse climbing under the covers beside me. I rolled onto my back and fell asleep as soon as my eyelids closed.

V

I awoke from a dream that smelled like a burning candle. Like rotting grass and iron blood poured into liquid wax, a wick run through it, set and hardened, lit aflame. The blinds had not been closed the night before and nothing blocked the feeble morning sun. Every limb felt impossibly difficult to move as if I were covered in chainmail.

My toes were stiff, legs like wooden poles, and my torso felt tender, as if I had been repeatedly punched in the stomach until the skin had become pulpy and bruised. I laid awake in a sleepy stupor for several minutes, my thoughts drawn to a dull ache between my legs. Period cramps, I thought to myself. But my period was at least two weeks away. I got up to pee, but couldn't, so I went back to bed. The female body was a mysterious entity to inhabit at times. I placed my left hand over my lower stomach and felt the warmth spread from my hand to the soft skin. Jesse was breathing heavily beside me, still asleep, and so I rolled over onto my side and watched his chest rise and fall with each breath. It was calming to see someone in total peace, asleep and unafraid, the body simply at rest.

The time was edging toward ten o'clock by then, and I needed to force my body out of bed, down the stairs, and into my car. Some alcohol still sloshed around in my system, yet I heaved my legs over the edge of the bed. I blew a kiss to Jesse and found a scrap of paper and a pen. I wrote a quick note to tell him I had gone home and left it beside the bed.

The stratus clouds in the sky were murky clumps of charcoal above me as I drove.

Mom was in the kitchen when I got home, busy at work, the scent of lemon dish soap and strawberry jam present.

"Good morning, sweetheart," she said. "How was your time at Anna's?"

I slipped off my shoes. "It was fine." I clenched my teeth. Until that moment I hadn't thought much about the previous night or the panic attack in the face of the more pressing problem that was my hangover. I hated wearing a mask in my parents' home. I hated choosing words carefully, stepping around the truth.

I could not possibly have written the essay I needed to. I collapsed onto my bed and dissolved into the familiar comfort of my childhood bed, happy that each shadow on the wall fell in its place. I was asleep in minutes.

A soft knock on the door came. "It's lunchtime," Mom's muffled voice filtered through to me.

I lay still.

It was March twentieth and therefore spring. One of the earliest records of tracking time was found in a small cave. Twenty-eight little lines were engraved in stone. Of course it was a woman who discovered calendrical time; it was in our bodies to understand the structure of time, we were inherently at one with nature. I found this to be divinely profound one morning as a teenage girl. It was comforting to be a part of the earth's timing. Even if I didn't like my body, I liked the vitality of womanhood.

After lunch I checked my phone and saw that Jesse had texted, asking when we would see each other next. *Tomorrow, ideally,* I texted back. I would need to forcibly create one thousand mildly academic words before then. It could be done, it wasn't impossible, and there was always coffee.

I cut up an apple and scooped almond butter out of a jar. I scraped the spoon with my teeth. Sticky mouthed, I went back to my room.

The afternoon slipped away, and I was shaken by a second tapping on the bedroom door.

Mom cracked open the door just enough to poke her delicately greying head through. Like leaves in the fall, her dark blonde hair was slowly changing colour. The flaxen gold was now streaked with soft grey. She did not believe in dyeing hair since it would be an act of defiance against the Lord himself, changing the hair colour he had given you. "Dad won't be here for dinner, and I know that you are busy with this essay right now, so I was wondering if I could bring you anything to eat?" she asked. She glanced down at the almond butter-streaked glass plate beside me. "Oh, here." Mom held out her hand.

That was Mom: intensely self-sacrificing and concerned for others' needs far above her own. I didn't understand how she could be so good. She bought the ingredients to make your favourite meal, she stayed up hours after everyone else had gone to bed to wrap Christmas presents, she sent cards in the mail just to say she was thinking of you. I had inherited her sensitive spirit, but I never believed that I could fully embody her selflessness.

I handed my mom the plate. "That would be nice."

"You look tired," she said.

"I am."

I could have mouthed her next words: "Did you not sleep well last night?" she asked. Mom was fixated on how well her loved ones slept, even though she often deprived herself of rest.

I lifted one shoulder in a shrug and mumbled something about it not being great.

"I'll bring you some food and then you can take a nap."

I didn't have time for a nap, but I smiled.

I took a Motrin for the discomfort I still felt in my stomach and legs, but it made me even more tired. And yet I was only home for twenty-four more hours, and the time needed to be used before the sand ran out, before Jesse and I had to leave our home base in opposite directions.

I was back in Jesse's kitchen later the following day, running my fingers through the copper brown hair that had grown to touch the nape of his neck. I repeatedly curled a lock around my index finger, liking the silky feeling. Jesse opened the door of the empty fridge then immediately shut it again. "Right. So, should we go out for dinner before I drive you back to the city?"

We drove to a diner that sat in the heart of a small town halfway between my parents' country home and my city residence. The gold of the diner's front door handle had rubbed off from years of hungry patrons. It was an hour until close, and the waitresses looked tired.

Jesse and I chose a booth by a large window. There were only two other people in the restaurant.

I looked through the sticky menu. "Anything that can be deep fried is," I said.

A waitress appeared at the tableside, and I watched as ice cubes crashed into our glasses from the pitcher she poured from. I ordered a veggie burger and sweet potato fries, Jesse ordered an all-day breakfast option. The waitress whisked our menus away.

"So," I said. "Forest boy."

"Yes, ma'am," Jesse quipped. He lifted the glass of water to his lips, the tips of his fingers and fingernails permanently browned from dirt. It didn't matter how much he scrubbed his hands with soap, still they carried soil.

"Did you miss me?" I touched his hand.

"Of course, kid."

We discussed summer plans and the possibility of me flying out west to visit.

A lady bug had crawled its way to the side of the booth and Jesse picked up a napkin to smoosh it.

"You kill ladybugs?" I asked, mildly horrified.

"They're bugs."

"They're friends and family."

50

I extended my leg out underneath the booth's table and playfully bumped his knee just as our server came marching toward us with food. I quickly retracted my leg and Jesse made quiet *tsk, tsk, tsk* sounds under his breath, his eyes glinting in the warm lighting, his mouth a brazen half smile.

Jesse scooped up an egg onto a piece of heavily buttered toast. The yolk slowly seeped out, thick and yellow. "What are you going to do after graduation?" he asked.

I sighed. "That is a good question. Six months ago, I was considering going right into a master's degree, but fourth year burnt me out. University is … counterintuitive for me sometimes. I can do it, but I can't do it like how they want me to do it."

I looked out the large window we were seated near and could see the waning crescent of the moon in the evening sky.

The hour ticked away and the waitress undoubtedly wanted us gone. I nervously tapped at Jesse's forearm. "We need to go," I said and reached for my purse, ready to throw down my credit card. Jesse calmly pushed my hand away. "Cool your jets, kid. I'll get it."

Jesse always paid the bill at restaurants in full. I had thought of it as considerate kindness, especially since I was still in university and he had graduated and was working a full-time job.

Once in a small pub, near the corner of Yonge and Adelaide, my assumption was slightly shaken as I walked toward Jesse and the bartender after having used one of the closet-sized washrooms. A little hazy wonderland had begun forming in my head from the two cocktails, one lavender-coloured and chilled with a perfect sphere of ice and one made too sweet with simple syrup and a candied twist of orange on the rim. Two tones of voices, one Jesse's and another one raspy, met my ears through the din as I climbed back onto my chair. They laughed in unison, the bartender handing Jesse a debit machine. The laughter broke and disintegrated into their throats quickly when I appeared. A small, but heavy mass sunk to the bottom of my stomach and remained there for the rest of the night. I never asked Jesse what words were spoken in case I would have rather not known.

The stars were out, cold white light in the velvet sky. Jesse and I were out of the diner, arm in arm, walking toward Jesse's truck, then past—I puttered to a halt. "Jesse, you passed the car."

A cheeky smile from Jesse, pink tongue peeking out from behind white teeth, and a gentle tug on my arm.

"What are you doing?" I laughed and feigned a little protest as I let him lead me down the sidewalk.

We crossed the street, two doors slid open, and a wash of fluorescent light enveloped us as aisles full of glass bottles stood before us. We darted toward the back of the LCBO and studied the canned alcohol. Tall, thin cans, short, squat cans. Tropical fruits, harsh neon, soft pastels, hops, seltzer, too many words. I sighed and pushed my face into Jesse's shoulder. "How can you want alcohol again after Anna and Kieran's? You choose one for me."

Jesse picked out a couple of drinks, I tagged along to the check out, and he handed me one of the cans once we were outside again. Hard seltzer—bubbly, dry, and sweet.

Then came the pleasant humming in my brain; the air nipping around our bodies now incidental. We sipped and hardly thought to be discreet with the drinks in the darkened empty streets. We walked down deserted sidewalks until we came to a small pond enclosed in the heart of the town park. Only a thin sheen of ice still clung to the edges of the water. The silhouettes of two Canadian geese roamed around the grounds, the streetlight illuminating the haughty black beady eyes.

I slipped my cold hand into Jesse's warm one. He never seemed to get cold or sick.

We walked along the pathways that wound throughout the park. Jesse's breath became plumes of condensation when he exhaled, and I found this endearing to watch. I turned my head slightly to kiss his shoulder and he squeezed my hand.

Jesse stopped walking as we came to a bench.

"Here, I'll warm you up, you cold-blooded thing," he said, sitting down and opening up his arms for me.

I sat down beside him, twisted my body sideways on the bench, rested my legs in a V-shape over his lap, and leaned my head on his shoulder. The north wind was biting, and yet I felt indifferent to the cold. The seltzer had formed a warm buffer between myself and the world.

"I don't want you to go," I said into Jesse's chest.

"I know," he said.

"I'll miss you."

"I know."

"I want you to come back before long."

"I know."

I felt his finger lifting my chin and his warm mouth met mine. The rhythm of his heart beat against my breast. I could feel his hand grasping at my hip and thigh, his arm curved around my back.

Footsteps on last year's dead leaves came down the pathway and Jesse and I pulled apart.

"It's already almost nine-thirty," I said as I flicked on my phone.

Jesse laughed and I lightly punched his arm. "Yes, that's late for me, shut up!"

Jesse pulled me along like I was a limp teddy bear until I was able to melt into a tired puddle on the passenger seat beside him.

I fought myself to stay awake. This was the last car ride with him for a while. *You'll want to think about this later,* I told myself. *Stay awake.*

Few headlights shone brightly past ours.

I woke up with the steering wheel just shy of my forehead. Jesse's hands were doing a wake-up jig on my arm. I had fallen asleep and gently keeled over onto Jesse's right knee.

"Wake up, kid," he whispered in my ear.

"No," I mumbled and hugged his leg with my arm.

"Well, I've turned off the engine and it's going to get cold in here soon."

"Turn it back on."

"No." Jesse's fingers kept dancing over my shoulder and arm.

"Fine," I said and heaved myself upright. "Can you stay a bit? Ten minutes?"

Jesse trailed after me into my apartment and we laid down on my bed.

"It makes me sad when you leave." I stated my feelings. I had begun doing this more. Naming emotions just as they were, in simplicity and sincerity, felt graceful and affirming.

"I know it's always difficult," Jesse said. "But I also know that after a few days the shitty feelings go away and you're back to normal."

I lifted my head up so that our features aligned. "Do you get sad too?"

"Yes," said Jesse. "But not in the same way I don't think. You lose all hope for like three days. I'm sad to leave, but I know I'll be back, so what's there really to feel sad about? I would only feel really sad if I thought I were leaving for good."

"Isn't the parting hard in and of itself? I know you'll be back, I know I'll see you again. But it's hard nonetheless and sometimes I can hardly stand it."

I would have rather had my right arm sawn off than experience the emotional pain of aching for someone. A branding iron, smouldering red, pressed against my skin. Insufferable aching.

Jesse did not understand the disordered aspect of who I was. He understood my anxiety disorder and depression to be akin to the usual anxieties and sad spells of the human experience, only I got more hung up on them. He was so innocently unaware.

Anxiety was felt by everyone and so most believed they had a grasp of the meaning of *anxiety disorder.*

Sometimes I felt I was a terminally ill patient sitting in a hospital waiting room between two patients who had a cold and a flu. One of the patients would slowly turn to look at me, my face ashen and distraught. As a warm smile spread across their face, the patient beside me would reach their hand out to gently pat my own. *Being sick is difficult, dear, I know,* they would say nodding wisely. I would move my gaze from their hand on top of mine up to their warm face. Too tired to say anything, I would simply nod, smile, and pat their hand right back.

I could not explain the difference between anxiety and an anxiety disorder without disclosing too much information or sounding insensitive or appearing to compare human pain. Therefore, I did not try.

I closed my eyes and kept my head rested against Jesse's chest. "Okay," I said. "I'll try to think about things less."

But I did not know how to think less. My mind was a violently disobedient child, overactive when it should be still, hypersensitive when it should remain calm. I needed eternal distraction. I read and invested in the plight of others. Memoirs were holy testaments. I consumed them as a necessity—as air, as love.

Fiction could be used as comfort too. I thought about the authors more than their characters. Some authors were lucid, omniscient, and omnipresent gods of their own making, knowing every minor detail of life, from their characters' first breath to their last. The reader moved along with the author's knowledge; little angels by their god's side witnessing their dominion.

And some authors were decidedly structured. There were self-imposed laws of nature between the front and back covers that the authors both created and abided by. Law and order in accordance with the passage of time existed.

One question demanded to be asked, at all times, no matter the book: *what did you hide between the lines, dear author?*

Jesse left for B.C. and my mind fell into a deep cavern and all was dark. I reached for the unread books I had stockpiled like they were medicine. One night as I lay in bed sweating, I considered calling my mom. I needed a voice to call me out of the cave. Instead, I texted Roslin my woes and fell asleep in a tangled heap of blankets.

Frost came again that night. Temperatures dipped down unusually low, and the spider webs of frost appeared on the edges of every window overnight. Every leaf and tree bud was delicately coated with crystals that refracted sunlight. I had not checked the weather and I was not prepared, so I shivered through the day and had bought a total of two teas and one coffee by the time the sun went down.

I slammed the door when I made it back home, which sent Victoria skittering out of her sleep. She had been toasting like a marshmallow beside the radiator.

If the ground had not hardened so much from the recent frost, I would have considered digging a hole and throwing myself in face first. Jesse's departure had been a tipping point that made the stress of exams and final papers all the more unbearable, and I simply wanted to plant myself in the dirt.

I flipped my desk calendar ahead to look at the coming days. I had all my exams marked in the little white squares. The end of term schedule was as follows: try, try, try, until I would break down and submit assignments while blinking back tears. It was an exhausting tradition that one had to complete eight times in a four-year program. Students could seek additional support from the accommodations department if they had verified forms filled out by a doctor or psychiatrist. By the end of my second year, it had become obvious I needed additional support.

A nauseating recollection convinced me to get help. The memories of restriction, the footsteps of the nurse on suicide watch, and the words gashed into the walls with human finger nails had all made it very clear to me. My physical heart had nearly suffered permanent damage—consequences of the damage in my metaphysical heart—after sixty blue and white pills had entered my bloodstream.

And so, never wanting to relive that memory, I walked through the doors of my psychiatrist's office, fist clutching medical forms embossed with the university's logo.

He perused the papers quietly. "What exactly should I be writing here?" he asked.

Mentally unable to cope with post-secondary life, I wanted to say. Instead, I told him what the university wanted: a confirmation of medical health problems and why they made academia hard.

My psychiatrist nodded and scribbled on the forms with his pen.

I woke on Thursday morning to sunshine trying to peep through the thick window curtains, the sunrays only making it through when warm air rising from the floor register blew the curtains gently apart.

My chest was aching already then. My heart felt strained and heavier than the rest of my body, as if gravity had specifically chosen that organ to apply more force to than necessary. It was the aching aftermath of saying goodbye, it was the overwhelming weeks ahead.

I got out of bed and pulled one curtain to the side. It had rained during the night and puddles dotted the road.

I came under the sudden conviction that I needed to go for a run and looked for my old white Nike running shoes. It would be the first time I wore them that year. I pulled the shoes out of my closet, slightly squashed down and deformed from the weight of other shoes that had rested atop them. Same sweat stains on the insoles from last season.

Long ago I had trained myself to un-focus my eyes when a mirror was in front of me. Like a camera lens bringing things in and out of focus, my eyes automatically blurred out the image in the mirror, and I did not look directly at my face. The clothes, the hair, yes, but never the face. When I looked in the mirror, I felt like I was looking at a colouring page where I had coloured outside of the lines, and my heart would sink to the floor.

While I stood in front of the mirror, I kept my gaze lifted upward to the bun I was fashioning my hair into.

My legs felt tight and sinewy, and they were shocked at what felt like blunt force trauma every time they hit the surface of the sidewalk pavement. The crisp air coated my lungs with each inhale. I didn't want to think and I didn't want to *be*. That's why I ran.

Why a human being? Why not a chrysanthemum, why not a jade-coloured luna moth? Why did I have to be a sentient being at all? Why could I not have simply been a stillborn, died in the womb, in the comfort of my mother.

These thoughts swirled while I waited for the barista to make my coffee, while the movie credits rolled, while the lights were still red.

I harboured many dreams and fantasies of dying, specifically dying as a child. These dreams were conjured up while I was both in depressive episodes and in stable moods.

I remember heat through a window pane hitting my face as a past therapist asked if I could imagine a future that would make dealing with my mental illness worthwhile. I looked directly at him, or rather in his general direction, as the sunlight blinded my vision.

"No. There is no future that would make this worthwhile," I said slowly and deliberately.

"Nothing?" came his voice from the human-shaped outline across from me.

"Nothing."

"How come?" He had asked.

"How come?" I leaned back. "Because when I think about that question, I am asking myself if I would live through what I have already lived through yet again, even if I knew that tomorrow would be the beginning of paradise. And the answer is no, never. I don't want to feel what I have felt ever again and saying that it would be worth it would be like discrediting my past self and all the torment she's been through." I looked up into the sun. "And then I think—" but my voice broke and I never finished that sentence out loud. But in my mind I finished it: *And then I think, well why go on now? Tomorrow will not be paradise, and I will still be sick.*

I had suppressed the tears welling up in my eyes. My therapist kept talking and did not seem to be aware that my eyes had turned into pools.

My legs began to harden themselves in response to the concrete beneath them. I didn't stop running until it was my lungs and not my legs that could not go on. Sweat stuck my hair to my temples and neck. I had not run in a circular way but had simply run without thinking further and further away from my apartment. With no money on me, I couldn't bus home or get a taxi, so I simply retraced my steps and regulated my breathing. Tried to outrun myself.

VI

I sat in front of an empty white screen, a tiny black vertical bar blinking, my mind its own little madhouse.

After an hour, words still refused to surface in my brain and a fire of frustration and anger stoked within me. I wanted to throw my laptop shattering through a window.

Several students had died by suicide at the university since I had enrolled. One had happened on the campus itself; the student threw themselves out of a window. I recoiled at the thought of a crumpled body being found, bloody and dead, somewhere on campus. Or had the suicide been witnessed? My mental illness envied all suicide victims. I imagined the body falling and what the hard cement did to it upon impact. What was it like to watch the ground rushing up to meet oneself? Which bones broke first? Did blood seep out like a crimson tide from underneath where the head lay? Were the eyes open or closed? I didn't want to know these things, and yet I did want to know. A nauseating curiosity about those who'd taken their own life simmered in the back of my mind.

I knew that most people would be scandalised, appalled, disgusted. Would explain exactly why you should not kill yourself. Because of how much it would hurt others. Ignorance suffocated empathy. I knew how to make them understand however. They would only need to be stabbed every day, just beneath their last rib, then asked, *now how many days would you like to go on like this? Not many more? Does that mean we should put you on suicide watch?* The physical manifestation of mental illness complete.

I thought about all these things as I climbed into a tepid shower. The water ran over my body, mingled with the grime of yesterday, and rushed it all down the bathtub drain. I washed my skin with cherry blossom-scented body wash. I massaged shampoo that smelled like sunscreen into my hair. My peripheral vision took note of my wrists as they moved through the water. I brought my left wrist in front of me for inspection. I contemplated the blue-green and purple-blue veins that spread out into three separate paths just before reaching my hands. How funny that we could see our veins beneath our skin. How easy it was to see where we could end the blood flow, our wrists hanging by our sides, day after day.

I got out of the shower and towelled off, my skin shivering slightly in the cooler air of my bedroom. I pulled a vintage band t-shirt over my head and light pink underwear over my legs, and then I put the kettle on for tea.

When I pulled into Sonya's long driveway later that day, Forest was there at the side of the house, her tail wagging so ferociously that it nearly sent her off balance.

"Hi, sweetheart," I whispered under my breath. Forest's mouth naturally fell into a smile. Huge chocolate-covered almond eyes looked up at my face, a pink tongue rested at the bottom of her happy mouth, and a small tuft of fur flew off her tail as it kept wagging.

"Sorry," I said to Sonya as Forest skipped past me and into the office the moment I opened the door.

"Oh, don't worry, she was due to come back in," Sonya said and ushered me inside.

The soft couch looked inviting to me now, the texture of each mismatched pillow known to me by then.

Sonya asked me her check-in questions. She rated my mood and emotions on a scale and asked if there was something in particular I was anxious about that day. She asked me about my energy levels, on a scale of one to ten, one being death-like exhaustion and ten being the energy of a six-year-old. I told her that I was at level three. Any lower felt overdramatic.

"Last time I saw you, your energy level was at a five," said Sonya. "Is there any reason it would be lower now?"

I shrugged. "The exhaustion is building up from university things I guess."

Sonya nodded and made a note in her papers.

"And," —I pulled one of the pillows into my lap as some sort of comfort— "My boyfriend was here visiting, and he left a few days ago. So …" I didn't want to go into detail. "So that sucks."

"I'm sorry, that must be hard," Sonya said. "We can talk about your boyfriend and how you're feeling about his departure in our session today if you would like. How have the panic attacks been?"

"I've had a couple since I was last here."

"Have they been triggered by specific thoughts or circumstances or did they happen randomly?"

"Specific thoughts and circumstances."

"And how have you felt during these panic attacks?" Sonya looked back in her notes. "You often describe the panic attacks as being paralyzed by fear. Is that how you felt again?"

I nodded and pulled the pillow tighter against my body. "Yes. Like that."

"At any point did the panic attacks make you wish to harm yourself or end your life?"

I always danced around this question like it was a bomb, assuring any therapist who asked that I wasn't *actively* suicidal. I just didn't want to be alive sometimes.

I would never breathe a word about the suicide note, now two years old, that was somewhere I could not remember.

"Not really," I said.

"Not really?"

"I mean, no, I haven't been suicidal." Not very, anyway.

Sonya absentmindedly leaned over and scratched Forest's head with her pen. "Have you felt able to lean on the support of friends and family since I last saw you?"

I thought of Jesse's blank eyes and agitated hands in Anna's bathroom. I let the stage curtains fall on that image and replaced Jesse's face with Roslin's. She understood well enough at least.

"I have," I said.

"Since I saw you last, have you posted the hotlines in a clearly visible or easy to access place?"

"Yes." But over my dead body would I have called any one of them.

Sonya folded her hands neatly. "Would you like to talk about how you've been feeling about your boyfriend leaving now?"

"Sure," I said, my voice arid.

"So, your boyfriend—" Sonya looked back in her notes "Jesse."

"Yes."

"He has gone back to B.C.?"

I imagined what she must have written down during my first appointment when she was gathering all the relevant information needed to map me out. What did people think of Jesse? I had no idea; I had been with him too long to know what he was like.

"He left just a few days ago."

"How do you feel about that?" Sonya asked.

"I'm missing him."

"How was his recent visit?"

"I guess it was good?" Wasn't it? "Yes, it was good," I said.

Sonya stayed silent which meant she was waiting for me to continue talking. Silence—a nasty trick used by therapists to draw out information from clients.

"I was really busy with school while he was here, so we probably spent less time together than usual. But we had a nice time, I think. We were together at his place, we went to a friend's party, and we actually went out on a date too. Like a *date* date."

Sonya smiled. "That sounds nice. What was the *date* date?"

"We went out for dinner and walked around a park afterward."

"Beautiful." She tapped her pen and Forest's ears twitched in her sleep. "Is Jesse aware of your health?"

I nodded.

"How aware?"

I wondered the same thing. "He knows I have anxiety."

"Does he understand that an anxiety disorder is different from having anxiety about things?"

Mind-reading counsellor, she had been in my head. "He's learning," I said, coming to the defence of my boyfriend. The panic attack last week may have shaken him. "I think Jesse understands that I have a lot of anxiety about a lot of things a lot of the time."

Sonya swirled her pen around on her notepad as she wrote, then set the pen down. "That is good and healthy that Jesse is aware. I have noticed a pattern when it comes to couples wherein one of the individuals has a mental illness diagnosis. Often the individual with the mental illness falls into one of two categories: one, they do their best to hide their mental illness from their partner, or two, they so desperately want their partner to understand their health issues but are afraid that it may be overwhelming for them to handle. There is a real need that those who suffer from mental illness have: they need to be *well understood* by their partners in a society that still does not understand this particular type of illness. Mental illness is still fundamentally misunderstood. I'm sure you're aware of this." Sonya's eyes met my own. "This may or not apply to you and your boyfriend, I do not know, but even if it doesn't, I think it is helpful to know that many people with mental illnesses find it difficult to be understood by their partners."

I nodded.

"It is very, and I mean *very*, important that those closest to someone with a diagnosed mental illness are educated about the illness. It will make life easier for both you and your partner if they grasp the reality of mental illness—and how yours affects your health, moods, and abilities."

I instantly wanted to shed tears over these kind words. Above all else I wanted to be understood. I wanted it to be understood that sometimes the falling evening shadows made my mood plummet into its own black shadow. I wanted it to be understood that my brain drowned in anxiety. I wanted it to be understood that I was scared of people getting angry at me for my many anxieties. I wanted it to be understood that I was hard to understand and that I was well aware of this.

"Now if I remember correctly, you had said that your parents are quite aware that mental illnesses are real health issues," Sonya continued. "And I remember you saying that you felt supported by them, which is good to hear. Imogen, it is your choice as to who you explain your health to, but I would like to make some suggestions."

Sonya paused and waited until I gave the go-ahead nod. "Your best friend Roslin should be well aware of your health. And your boyfriend of three years should be well aware of your health also. It is not your responsibility to educate them. The burden does not lie on you, Imogen. The only responsibility you have is to be transparent with Roslin and Jesse about your diagnoses and how it affects your life. Share as much as you comfortably can and then tell them that it is important that they understand your health issues. And then that's it. You've done your part."

I wasn't looking at Sonya, I fixed my eyes on Forest's rib cage as it rose and fell with each of her unconcerned breaths, trying not to cry.

"Can you do that, Imogen?" Sonya asked.

"Yes." I swallowed. "I think so."

"It may be difficult, but ultimately life gets easier when those close to you understand who you are. It really does."

"I want to tell you something else," said Sonya. "It would be good if your loved ones were aware of anxiety coping techniques. However, people should never weaponize anxiety coping techniques against you. Sometimes, despite the best of intentions, people can use the things that are meant to help alleviate anxiety to guilt and hurt those with the mental illness. If someone is expecting you to function better because there are anxiety coping techniques available, then this is replacing love, patience, and understanding. Sometimes there is frustration and disapproval shown toward a mentally ill person when they are not trying hard enough to use coping methods. Instead of the coping methods being helpful, they are being used against you. Does this make sense?

I bit my lip until I tasted blood. I knew exactly what she meant and had never heard someone speak the sentiment so clearly. A little firefly lit up in my chest and fluttered through my ribs.

"I have known people who have not wanted to come to therapy because their partner or a family member has *expected* the therapy to improve their mental health. There is a fear that the partner or family member will be frustrated with them if they come to therapy and their health doesn't improve. As I've said before," Sonya clicked off her pen. "People do not have the right to make you feel badly for having an illness. Remember that as well."

I curled up in a tight ball underneath all the bed covers as soon as I got home from Sonya's and slept for two hours. When I awoke, I stayed in my apartment physically, but mentally I went to sit on a low ledge in a make-believe field of wildflowers, long grass, and weeds. I swung my legs back and forth, feet grazing the wild garden below me. My toes ran through a small spray of periwinkle-blue flowers. I did not know their name though I had seen them many times before. But somewhere there were books with the flowers' names in them, and they were written about and studied and drawn, and they must be someone's favourite flower. The entire field before me was full of flora that had been studied by botanists. I smiled because all the little plants and their little stems and leaves were rather important, with different accoutrement and methods of living.

I stumbled back down to Earth and found I was still in my bed.

There were deadlines to meet, and so I wearily left the horizontal. I tried to study and told myself to manage.

The appointment that morning with Sonya was playing over and over again in my head. Jesse needed to know more about my health. I did not fear outright rejection or a breakup. Far worse than either of those things would be a blank void behind his eyes, him minimizing the severity of my health or not comprehending how he could help. I did not think that Jesse would melt down or recoil. The cruellest fate would be a passive nod, a mild acknowledgement, a failure to grasp my reality. I was sure that after telling my boyfriend one of the foundational pillars that shaped who I was, he would nod and say, *I see,* though he did not. I felt so much. How did Jesse feel so little? Had he learned to suppress feelings at a young age, nipping them at the bud, killing the fruit of humanity?

Soft artificial blue light illuminated my room. Jesse was sending text messages, asking me how my day was, telling me he would be in a region with patchy cell service for the next few days.

That's fine, stay safe, I messaged back. I imagined Jesse in the middle of hundreds of towering trees that banded together to block out cell service. *Jesse, could we schedule a time for a phone call?* I typed out, but my fingers paused, I deliberated. The conversation we needed to have would be better to have in person, and it would likely have a greater impact that way. But I doubted that Sonya would think it wise for me to wait until Jesse was home again to have the conversation. That could push the conversation months down the road.

Still, I deleted the text message.

The next day: tired, again. I was so tired I wanted to cry. I wanted to stretch the nighttime out like bubble gum, double the length. Sleep for eighteen hours, only need to be awake for six. And I did accidentally manage this by falling asleep immediately after turning off my alarm and promising myself that I would get out of bed at any moment.

When I finally got up, I ate a Gala apple and reached into my closet for my spring jacket. Time for a run. Walking out my apartment door sometimes felt like breaking the seal of a bottle or popping a bubble. The little world dissipated, the larger world engulfed. People were in this outside world. Lime green traffic lights, orange school buses, broken homes, gorgeous mansions—they were all out there.

Fresh cold air blew through my hair like icy tentacles. I shut all other functions down within myself besides the motion of putting one foot in front of the other.

When I ran over the railroad tracks that crisscrossed throughout the city, I eyed them like someone eyes their secret crush, trying to get its attention, make a connection.

I nearly laughed as I glanced to my left and saw a provincial sign attached to the grey chain-link fence that ran along the sidewalk. Right at the railway crossing was posted a 1-800 suicide hotline number. *We're here to talk,* the sign read.

I studied the walls of the lecture hall like I was committing them to memory. This was the last class of my undergraduate. I had spent four years of my life on campus, and now this was the last class.

Three girls sat in front of me and whispered about a birthday party, pastel frosting, vodka shots, and dollar store confetti. The party seemed to be slated for that evening. They would be going out birthday partying around the same time I would be headed to Sonya's.

Class ended and that was the end of it, unceremoniously and abrupt, the glass doors of the Arts building folded behind me.

Sonya had a cancellation that week and could see me on Thursday afternoon. And I was happy to go. Walking into the crisp white office, with its contradictorily harsh architectural lines and yard sale rejects, was a natural function for me by then.

Forest's soft furry head, thinking only dog thoughts, would turn toward me in happiness whenever I sat down across from her and Sonya. Sonya was my counsellor, but I looked at Forest when I couldn't look Sonya in the eye.

When I got back to my apartment later that evening, I set my backpack and purse down as the soft, clear silence of home welcomed me back.

I smiled at Victoria who sat on the windowsill. She was an introvert at heart herself and enjoyed the clarity that came with solitude. Victoria would sometimes pad her way into the shadows of my closet, sit down, encircle all four paws with one long tail, and gaze pensively outward, collecting her thoughts that were few and far between.

On Thursday, I reined in my car to a halt and berated myself for the over dramatics that had caused me to ask Sonya for an earlier appointment. I had booked the appointment in the throes of a particularly dark day, but when the appointment day came, I felt altogether neutral and frighteningly normal. I had attended the last lecture of my undergraduate studies and now that was done. I felt accomplished, and this momentarily lightened the darkness. The need for the early appointment was silly and unnecessary.

I sat down on the toffee-coloured couch, seating myself on the same third of cushions as I always did.

Sonya was wearing a headband, her hair far less styled than usual. I wondered if she truly had an appointment cancelled or if she had carved out this hour specifically for me.

The couch felt so warm and familiar, I could have curled up right there and hibernated for a week or two.

Sonya smoothed out her calf-length pleated skirt and flipped open my file, ready to counsel me.

The regular check-in questions ensued and I answered them all in a cool, moderate tone. There had been no need for an emergency appointment.

The person I would describe to therapists felt like an abstract image that couldn't quite fill the shape of me. There was a little shift, a stepping outside of oneself to become a cleaner version in the presence of a professional. This happened without trying. It made the person I was describing from the week before look odd and unmanageable. I was a snake describing the skin I had shed.

I watched as Sonya flipped through several pages.

"It seems that your energy level consistently scores very low in our check-ins," Sonya said. "I would say that you have a serious ongoing issue with fatigue."

"One might say that," I said.

"Have you ever been treated for exhaustion or chronic fatigue before?"

"I haven't."

Sonya lifted her slight hand to her mouth and delicately chewed at a nail. "I think you should consider getting some blood work done, Imogen."

I thought not. Needles made me ill. "Okay," I said.

"Blood work can show us if there are deficiencies contributing to your extreme fatigue."

"Okay," I said again, ironically too tired to tell her how much I despised the idea of someone purposely pushing steel through my skin and into my bloodstream, though I had thought of doing the same thing to myself many times, but for very different reasons.

Sonya then assumed the task of ascertaining why I had emailed her in a panic, asking for an appointment as soon as possible. But I felt numb to *those* feelings.

This phenomenon was not uncommon, and in the aftermath of the dark days, I would be left questioning why I had overshared and had needed so much support at the time. When darkness lifts, one always forgets just how dark it was. When the light is switched on and you can see where to walk, one thinks, well, really, how hard could that have been in the dark?

"Everything is too much. Just everything, you know? Getting out of bed, keeping a clean and tidy apartment, deciding what to eat." I had a thimble-full of precious energy each day. *Everything*, every breath, every task, every commonplace activity was a tax on that thimble-full. It may have been that I was a lower-grade mammal accidentally zipped up into the human body. I hated the human world and I didn't want to be a part of it. I had not asked to be there and I held a grudge against whatever act of fate or providence that had orchestrated my arrival.

"Whatever it is that triggers the anxiety is incidental. If it makes you feel anxious, then it makes you feel anxious," said Sonya. "I am here to help you manage your anxiety and develop methods to rise above the anxiety that is debilitating, but you never ever need to feel badly about what makes you anxious. Okay?"

"Okay," I said quietly.

"As I have said before, mental health is still so widely misunderstood, and so there are certain burdens that those who have mental illnesses are made to feel they need to bear. Try your best to identify false guilt that will only make your anxiety and depression worse, and set that guilt aside."

Sonya continued since I remained silent. "I am sorry that you happen to be living in a time period that is still virtually in the dark ages of mental health. Yes, there are medications now, less stigma than there once was, but believe me, we are still in the dark ages. Are you aware of the Accessibility for Ontarians with Disabilities Act?"

"No, I'm not," I said.

"Well, the AODA was put into place to ensure that anyone with a disability could access services and could not be discriminated against by employers. Do you know when the AODA was made into law?" She paused briefly. "2005. That's how recently we've decided to legally acknowledge that people with disabilities are entitled to the exact same accessibility as any other citizen."

I nodded along as Sonya spoke. I liked when she explained things, went into detail about something she was passionate about.

"So, we've decided that someone who, for example, is in a wheelchair needs the same access to the world as non-wheelchair people. Businesses have to be wheelchair accessible now; disabilities like that are increasingly being accounted for. But I am sad to say that mental health accommodations are largely still up in the air." She took a breath. "You say that your university has accommodations for those with physical disabilities and mental health issues?"

"Yes. Some."

"Well, that's good. That's some progress, and, I would assume, fairly recent progress. The point I'm trying to make is that we are living in a time where scientific research has only just begun to look at mental health, and a hundred years from now, people will look back to today and be shocked about the ignorance that surrounded mental health, just as we are now shocked and sorry for the insane asylums and psychiatric treatments from days gone by. So, I want you to know that it is the state of modern medicine, it is society, and it is ignorant, uneducated people that are problematic and need to improve, not you."

A little lump of emotion nestled itself in my throat.

Sonya continued. "Never ever add guilt or anxiety to your plate because of the ignorance of others. I would never want someone in a wheelchair to feel guilty for the inconvenience—" Sonya made air quotes, "—of a disability or any aid they may require. And it would be monstrous and inexcusable for someone to make them feel badly about being in a wheelchair. The same goes for your health," Sonya said in a tone of finality. "You're okay, Imogen, you are."

"I hate crying," I said as I started crying. I had not cried in a counselling session with Sonya before.

Forest shifted her warm almond eyes to my face and lifted her brow in that mildly inquisitorial way dogs do. I believed she was wondering what was wrong. She must have perceived humans to be an extremely delicate species after witnessing so many crying clients in her house.

"It's alright," Sonya said calmly. "Crying is healthy."

I grabbed a couple of tissues from the Kleenex box that constitutionally must be on the coffee tables in every counsellor's office.

I tried to build a dam of the white tissue under my eyes to halt the tears, but the tissue merely became soaked through. It was embarrassing and worst of all, Sonya remained deathly silent and let me cry. Only my muffled whimpers and small shuddering inhales could be heard. By then, Forest had lost all interest entirely.

Why was I crying? Had no one ever told me it was okay to be mentally ill before?

Fix it, said a voice that had hissed at me from the pit of snakes. *Fix yourself.*

Pleasant faces were picked up like masks and sickly-sweet smiles were cast in one's direction for the opening act as the orchestra played an inviting melody. People were there to talk and listen for a little while. And then the lights would dim until only you stood illuminated in a circle of light. You would be blinded momentarily and disoriented until you blinked your eyes like a newborn baby and saw the masks on the floor and the real faces of the people distort and shrink back into nothing. And the hiss of snake-voices remained.

I continued to cry while Sonya remained present, observing, but without any judgement.

"Remember the bloodwork and checkup," Sonya softly called out after me as I slipped through her door after the hour was up. "Just call Dr. Allis." My mind hiccupped when it heard my doctor's name in Sonya's mouth. But of course Sonya had this information. I had given it to her. It was always oddly disconcerting to have someone sitting opposite of you with a list of facts about you, both personal and frivolous, while you had nothing on them, save their housekeeping methods.

VII

Reward systems were essential. Go to an appointment, get a treat, Pavlovian conditioning. I cut up watermelon into bite-sized pieces with a large knife before my doctor's appointment, stashing it in the fridge for later. The reward.

I zipped into my black spring jacket and picked up my purse. Time to shine.

I arrived early to the appointment because I was afraid of being late. I remained in the car to wait out some time. I parted my hair directly down the middle, French braiding one half and then the other. I sorted through old receipts I had hastily shoved into my purse.

I went into the clinic, now only fifteen minutes early for the appointment, and let the receptionist know I was there, Imogen Waterhouse, for bloodwork.

An immediate head rush of light-headedness followed as I stood up abruptly like a soldier when the nurse called my name.

The nurse led me to one of the little hospital rooms, and I put a smile on my face as I answered all her questions. She asked me what medications I was on, and I had the names and dosages on the tip of my tongue. I often had to think about it for a minute or two since I had been on a variety of medications, some at the same time, with many dosage adjustments, my brain a little chemical laboratory.

The nurse, Monica, smiled sweetly as she left the room. The bloodsucking bloodletter would be with me shortly, she told me, though not in those words. Visions of blood draining from a vein in my arm left me lightheaded and cotton-mouthed.

The blood person came into the room wearing white scrubs, which was brave for someone working with staining red liquid. She leaned in to tie the marine blue rubber band around my upper arm.

No, thank you, I thought.

Smudges of black pushed into my field of vision.

"Can I lay down?" My panic asked.

"Oh. Sure," the woman said and stepped aside so I could get to the table lined with crinkly white paper.

I had determined that I would stand up and walk to the table like a healthy biped mammal, but my mobility was compromised.

The tall white blur beside me gently grasped my arm and supported me as I climbed onto the table.

The needle went in, the blood was drawn, the woman's scrubs remained snow-white, and I remained conscious.

I was fragile like a dried flower, and so I did what dried flowers do: curled up and hoped nothing would touch me that day that would make me fall apart. I faded into sleep.

It was seven o'clock in the evening when I opened my eyes again. The sun was sinking and cast a golden glow on the walls, on the old refrigerator I could see from my bed, on the quilt on top of me.

I begrudgingly left my love, my bed, and checked for new emails. My professor had sent a mass email saying he had messed up by including some incorrect study guidelines from the class he had taught the previous term. I had not started studying for the exam and was unaffected.

A receptionist from the doctor's office called, her light and syrupy voice telling me that Dr. Allis could see me yet that week to go over the blood test results.

The little blobs and globs of blue and yellow fish darted around the large aquarium in the waiting room of the doctor's office. Their bugged eyes and frenzied swimming patterns entertained me until a nurse wearing psychedelic cotton scrubs called *Imogen!* It was lovely that at least one vocation had escaped social norms and could have anything under the sun printed on their uniforms.

The nurse sat me down and asked me to state the reason for my visit, even though they were the ones who had made the appointment. She poised her pen above my file, ready to add another ailment.

"I'm really tired," I said. "I mean, that's why I'm here. I deal with extreme fatigue."

"I'm sorry to hear that," the nurse said in a monotone voice as she quickly jotted down what may have been, *she's really tired.*

I looked at the tiny sink in the corner of the room, the fire escape map on the wall, the white and grey flecked tiles on the floor.

"Does this fatigue disrupt daily life?" The nurse asked.

"Yes, quite a bit. I have anxiety and depression—" I glanced down at my file. And you could read all about it there, in a list that spliced together diagnoses and hospital visits and prescription drugs. "I know that fatigue is a symptom of those things, but lately it's been worse."

"Mm," the nurse murmured.

"So," I continued. "My counsellor suggested that I get bloodwork done and make a doctor's appointment to see if anything else might be wrong or contributing to the exhaustion."

"Yes, good. Well, Dr. Allis will be in shortly. She'll go over the results of the bloodwork with you, and you can go over the fatigue issue." And with that, the nurse was out the door, the psychedelic outfit in motion.

I had been in a doctor's office many times, but only on a few occasions had I been without my mom. It felt natural that one's mother would be in a little hospital room with them; she had made the body after all, if something were the matter with it, she would be there to hear about it.

However, this appointment was straightforward: I was only telling a doctor that I was a very tired person.

Dr. Allis sailed into the room like a little sparrow landing on a tree branch. Her short stature took a seat as the golden sunlight that beamed in through the small window glanced off her pin-straight white bob.

"Hi, Imogen," Dr. Allis looked at me and smiled warmly as though I were a friend. "It's good to see you, how are you?"

Dr. Allis was beautiful; she was in her late fifties and beautiful. Every appointment with her had me silently praying to age as she was. Trim and proper, Dr. Allis resembled the middle-aged women you would see in commercials pretending to be decades older than themselves and needing a retirement home.

"I'm doing alright. Well—" I paused. "—I mean, I'm here though, so …"

Dr. Allis smiled again, white teeth matching her hair. "I see that you are here because of an ongoing issue with fatigue?"

I subconsciously went to twist the plain gold band that had been my grandmother's wedding ring, but the finger was bare. I had mistakenly left it at Jesse's house, yet I always felt the ghost of it where it should have been.

"How many hours do you typically sleep each day?" asked Dr. Allis.

I wanted to say that that was a personal question since the answer was too embarrassing and pathetic. "Maybe fourteen? Sometimes more, sometimes less." If I had more time to sleep, I would. I was always trying to get the all-consuming exhaustion out of my bones.

"And do you ever feel rested?"

"No."

"Always exhausted?"

"Yes."

"Hm." Dr. Allis flipped through a few pages of my file. "You're on four milligrams of clonazepam."

"Yeah."

"And you've been dealing with exhaustion before clonazepam?"

"Yeah."

"I see. And have you ever had a sleep study done?"

"Sorry?"

"A sleep study. There are sleep clinics that you can go to where they monitor your sleeping over the course of one night to determine if you have a sleep disorder."

"Oh, I see."

"Has anyone ever noticed that you are restless in your sleep?"

"I sleep by myself mostly. But when I do sleep with my boyfriend, he hasn't ever said anything about me being a restless sleeper."

Dr. Allis nodded. "I think it would be best to book an appointment with a sleep clinic and have them conduct a sleep study on you."

"Who conducts the study?"

"Sleep technicians."

A neat title. I would be a prime patient since I could offer so many hours of study for them.

"Now," said Dr. Allis, setting aside my thick file. "We can go over the results of the bloodwork you had done a few days ago."

I smiled expectantly.

"All your levels look good. There is nothing to indicate that your exhaustion is a result of any particular deficiency."

My smile faltered. I had been secretly hoping that Dr. Allis would say, *of course you've been exhausted, you've had a deficiency in such and such. Please take this supplement and you will feel much better soon.*

"So, the good news is that your bloodwork shows you are healthy."

"Okay."

Dr. Allis folded her elegant hands in her lap, hazel eyes peering into my own. "Are you pregnant, Imogen?"

"No," I shook my head. "I'm not."

"No, Imogen, you are."

"What?" My mind floundered. "No, I meant to say that I'm not. I am not pregnant."

"Alright, but I said that you are pregnant."

"What?" I broke eye contact and fastened my field of vision onto the peach-beige wall across from where I sat, tracking invisible words that ran across the wall, as one's gaze would track a passing train.

"Blood work can give us pregnancy results. And the results show that you're pregnant, Imogen."

Thoughts and feelings were melting together into a molten lava, then seething through my veins as one rush of impact. I was hopelessly entrenched in my thoughts, my hearing hardly being one of the functioning five senses. *Dr. Allis had asked "Are you pregnant, Imogen?" Had she not? And I had altered the syntax of her sentence? Are you pregnant, Imogen? You are pregnant, Imogen.* The question and statement piled up one on top of another in my mind, like waves hitting sand, continuously, ceaselessly, to no end.

"I am not pregnant," I said.

Concern began to etch its way into Dr. Allis's features, the curved eyebrows pulled slightly downwards, the eyes mellowed with pity.

"Blood tests allow us to examine levels of hCG, which is highly accurate in determining pregnancy." She hesitantly rested a hand on my knee for a brief moment. "Imogen?"

But I wasn't really in the body she touched. *I'm not here, I'm not here,* was the impossible chant.

"Imogen. I assume this is an unplanned pregnancy?"

"Yes," I responded quickly.

"And you are aware that you have options?"

"Yes." I was briefly pulled back into the current flow of time, enough to feel the full impact of grief and anxiety like a sonic boom. I did not care that I was in front of a doctor, in public, I let my head sink into my waiting hands. Trapped in terror and enveloped in fear, I froze in that position, crystalizing.

I heard Allis's soft voice say, "I will provide you with resources and information. I know this can be a scary event, but many women go through these feelings, and I want you to know that you're not alone."

The wind was picking up and the waves of panic were getting larger, crashing in harder, and within my chest, I could feel a panic attack blossoming.

"How could I be pregnant?" I asked, stupid with denial.

"You mentioned a boyfriend?" Dr. Allis said.

Jesse had been with me in March, and we'd had sex five times while he was home. Jesse and I had used protection all five times; therefore, I was not pregnant; therefore, the blood test was wrong.

"You said you had a boyfriend, Imogen?"

"*Have* a boyfriend, yes," I replied through a shuddering exhale, before realizing that she had not been implying he was in the past. I was mishearing everything.

"You have a boyfriend. So …" she continued gently, leading me along the line of logic, "… you had sex about three or four weeks ago?"

"Yes. About three or four weeks ago."

"Well," said Dr. Allis. "The fetus is three to four weeks old according to the hCG levels in your blood test results. Imogen, are you okay?" The blurred white form of Dr. Allis asked. Snow white hair, pale white skin, impeccably white lab coat.

Her face crumpled into worry as she looked in my direction.

I was trying to leave the reality I was experiencing, splitting my consciousness from my body like splitting an atom.

And then suddenly the doctor in front of me came into focus more clearly, and I wanted to throw myself at her. She had been my doctor for years, and I had been to the doctor's office many times. She was one of the first people on the planet to know I was mentally ill, forging with me a strange, intimate bond. Dr. Allis felt like a close friend's mother, familiar and stable. Her life seemed so pristine and straightforward. I wanted to go home with her. I imagined her home to be a place of order and calm, zen and success, a place where problems could be solved. I wanted her to tell me what to do. *What do I do with a fetus? What do I do with a fucking fetus?*

I stood up and rushed to the small hand-washing sink on the other side of the office. I dry heaved and stabilized my weight with my arms on either side of the sink.

In a way, I had gotten what I wished for: the imminent panic attack was taking me out of reality and out of the Milky Way galaxy. It pushed me into the eye of a blackhole where time ceased to exist. There was only terror, that singular element, distilled into venom and invading my bloodstream.

I heard Dr. Allis rushing to my side, putting her hand on my shoulder, saying words into my left ear.

"I don't want to be here," the words rushed out without permission. Hot tears splattered into the metal sink.

"Do you want to go to the bathroom down the hall?" asked Dr. Allis.

"No," I heard my pitiful voice saying. "I don't want to be here, I can't." My legs collapsed and I slid down the side of the medical cupboards and onto the tiled floor. Tears streamed in rivulets down my face. I felt like dying, but only my mind was encased in the feeling of dying—I still had to live.

Dr. Allis knelt down on the floor beside my huddled body. To her, I was only a patient—a young woman who had gotten into the mess of an unplanned pregnancy, distraught and inconsolable on her floor. The young woman would eventually need to get up and leave. I would soon be gone, and Dr. Allis would remain in the clinic, white hair in place, greeting the next patient with a smile, driving home to a beautiful meal on white dishes and a conservative serving of red wine.

"I don't want to be here," I said again. "I don't want to do this."

And then Dr. Allis had a dilemma on her hands: was her patient, with a history of mental illness and one suicide attempt, so distraught that she needed immediate help? Did she need to go to a psych ward? Did she deem the girl to be at risk of self-harm?

"Is there someone you would like me to call? Someone who could pick you up and be with you?" she asked.

"No, it's alright, it's okay. I just need to stop crying, and then I can leave," I said.

"But I don't want you leaving my office if you're feeling unstable or …" Dr. Allis stood up. "Or if you are a danger to yourself."

I did not like the direction the conversation was heading and knew I needed to shut down. I could not be informed I was pregnant *and* being admitted to the psych ward on the same day.

I sniffed and took shuddering breaths, rapidly wiping at the stream of tears that seemed to know no end as Dr. Allis held out a box of thin, scratchy medical office tissues. I grabbed at the tissues and tried to dam up the flow of salty water, as the unforgiving tissues scraped away at my burning cheeks.

After two or three minutes I stopped crying, very suddenly and despite my efforts. One last shuddering breath, and then I felt my emotions die down like an old TV screen shutting off.

I got up off the floor and brushed off my jeans. "I'm okay now," I said.

"Are you sure?" Dr. Allis put the tissue box back in its place.

"I'm good. Really. It was just a shock."

"Alright, well, do you mind sitting again? I'm sorry, but I should just inform you of one more thing."

I sat.

"There are some medications we generally don't recommend women to take if they are pregnant. And clonazepam is one of them. I need to inform you that if you choose to keep the baby, we would recommend you go on a different medication."

"Oh." My eyes felt suddenly dry. "Thank you, that's good to know."

"You can call the clinic anytime to make an appointment, and we can look into a different medication for your anxiety then."

I appreciated her nomenclature of teamwork, regardless of how delusional it was. It was only me.

"Are you feeling better now?"

"Yes." I bent down to pick up my purse. "I'm feeling better."

"You are, really?"

I told my face to form a faint smile. "Really, I'm okay."

"Alright, well—" Dr. Allis's own faint smile formed "—I'll see you soon."

"See you soon," I walked out of her office and through the clinic's hallways, or at least I must have because then I was in my car, then buckling up the seatbelt, then starting the engine. I drove home, though I didn't remember any of that either. I must have put my foot on the gas at green lights and pressed the brakes at red ones.

I saw Victoria's heart-shaped face in the window as I pulled into my driveway, and the floodgates opened again. Victoria was a part of *my own life,* and now I had just brought the news of my pregnancy home. It was mixed into my real life. At the clinic I wasn't really me—you're never really you in foreign places—but now I was in my driveway in front of my door, key in hand, Victoria placidly staring through the window at me, and now I was me, and I was pregnant.

I went to my bedroom and sat on the edge of an unmade bed. After some time, I stood again, lifted up my shirt, and looked down. Nausea climbed up my throat like the climbing vines of deadly nightshade and blossomed in my mouth. Something alien was in my stomach.

I rushed to the bathroom and threw up into the toilet bowl, expelling nearly nothing since I hadn't eaten yet that day. I lifted up my shirt again in front of the bathroom mirror and continued to stare at the skin over my stomach that looked as it always had looked.

"Get the fuck out," I finally whispered.

A new cocktail of emotions—despair, anguish, and desperation—pulled me into my small kitchen. I opened one of the top cupboards, and stood on my tippy toes. I was looking for the piece of glass. The glass shard was a remnant of a set of four glass cups my mother and I had found before my first year of university, when I was just about to leave the nest. All four cups broke in one way or another, and it was only this piece, now dusty and rimmed with dried blood, which remained in a corner of the cupboard. I turned on the tap and ran water over the glass shard. How that was supposed to sanitize it, I didn't know, and I didn't care.

I held the piece of glass loosely in my hand and went to my bed, sitting down at the edge, exactly where I had been before. I took a breath and ran the glass crossways over the top of my thigh. It wasn't a deep cut, just enough to break the skin. Little beads of blood formed, small bright red circles hugging the cut lines. I focused on the cherry red colour, nothing else, not Victoria getting into mischief in the bathroom, not the sirens of an ambulance passing by, not the fetus inside me.

The small beads of blood joined one another and started to follow the pull of gravity and trickle down my thigh. I dabbed at the tiny streams with my fingertips and brought my hand upward to my nose, smelling iron-blood.

Rarely did I cut myself. It was sacredly kept for days of despair.

If a palm reader or fortune teller had told me I would commit suicide before I reached the age of twenty-five, I would have shrugged, slid my hand out of their grasp, and said, *that's weak, tell me something I don't know.*

That prediction would not have bothered me; the scale that measured living and dying already weighed heavily in favour of dying. But I did not know the scale would bend even further to that side.

There weren't cohesive thoughts then, only intangible emotions. It was me bleeding in the quiet of twilight and then realizing that I had cut too much, and that there was too much blood, and that I needed a box of Kleenex to stop the flow. It was just me, for the second time that day, feeling boiling hot tears fall down my cheeks, leaving those dry, salty rivulets on one's face that makes the skin tight and tired.

"It hurts," I whispered. The sentiment may have been about the six slits that now ran across my left thigh, but even I didn't know.

Almost out of Kleenex and still bleeding, I pressed a new sheet of tissue against my thigh and limped to the kitchen, where

I grabbed a roll of paper towel. I pressed paper towel after paper towel against my thigh as I got sleepy. I was cold and wanted to pull the blankets on my bed up to my chin, but I was scared of them coming in contact with the blood, and so I merely covered the right half of my body and lay back on my pillow, still holding a paper towel with force against my left leg.

When I woke, the wad of paper towels lay crumpled on the floor beside my bed, the dried blood made to look black in the dark room. I pulled my left leg under the covers and rolled over.

Morning came, dull and cloudy. Hazy dread, the residual coating of a dream I awoke from. Ten more minutes of rest was needed. Then a run, then a shower, hot breakfast—oatmeal maybe, with the raspberries that would soon sprout mould—

Like a drowning victim my face had broken the water's surface for a reprieve of oxygen, my mind had slipped into the dream world, but then I was plunged back into reality, the current pulled me down, deep under the water of memory.

I slapped my hand down to my left thigh and felt the ridges of six lines.

Shit. Shit, shit.

"Victoria," I called out, like a sad child calling for her mother, but it was me: a twenty-four-year-old woman calling for her pet. I needed something, someone, some living thing outside of myself.

I stared at the ceiling in a trance until I heard the padding of Victoria's small paws come my way.

By evening, I still had not studied a solitary minute for my exam the following afternoon.

Sometime in the middle of the night my eyes opened. The streetlight caused dimly shaped shadows to huddle beside the bedroom furniture. I awoke with a resolution running through my veins: I was not pregnant, I could not be pregnant because Jesse and I had used protection. The blood test was wrong, so very wrong. My hand flew to my phone sitting on the nightstand beside my bed. I asked the Internet how often blood tests were incorrect. A warm stream of hope began to trickle throughout my body, first in my mouth, then down to my chest, then to my stomach, and clear into my toes. Lab mistakes happened; it was not unheard of.

This was a *mistake*.

"Foolishness," I whispered into the shadows.

I fell back asleep.

Upon waking in the morning, I immediately picked up my phone again. I looked for the store hours of the nearest pharmacy. It would be open by the time I reached it.

I slid into leggings and an oversized vintage tee shirt, pausing to look down and whisper, *you motherfucker,* to my stomach before pulling the shirt all the way down.

You motherfucker, scaring me like that.

How funny it would be to have ended my life the day before, only for an autopsy to show an empty uterus. Like Romeo believing Juliet to be dead when she was merely asleep and drinking poison in his anguish while the omniscient reader says, *you fool.*

I raced to the pharmacy, and that peculiar air of being one of the first customers of the day hung in the air. I found the aisle with condoms and pregnancy tests. This was an unusual aisle for me to be in, and I was all at once self-conscious. Jesse was the condom-buyer. I had never bought a box of condoms in my life, and I had never so much as glanced at the pregnancy tests.

Pink, blue, and white boxes encased the thermometer-like sticks of plastic. Name brands and off-brands. There was First Response and Clearblue. A baby's laughing face on one of the boxes turned my stomach.

I bought two tests: one to make sure I wasn't pregnant and the other to make even more sure.

This was not an old pharmacy, and several self-checkout machines looked like shining beacons in my eyes. I did not want to be a girl walking through a checkout with two pregnancy tests and nothing else. I slipped both boxes into a plastic bag, paid, and walked quickly to my car.

Never again, I thought to myself, driving home. *Never again will I go through this nightmare. I will be so, so careful.*

I didn't have to pee immediately. I filled a glass to the brim with water and drank it, then sat down.

I sat still until my eyes widened in horror as it dawned on me that I had an exam to write that evening. This fact had been eclipsed entirely by the possibility of a poppy seed-sized fetus. I closed my eyes. I just needed to pee, take this test, put the pregnancy scare behind me, and then I would be grateful to study microeconomics all day long.

I took the boxes into the bathroom and ripped out the two tests, laying them side by side on the sink beside the toilet. I peed on both sticks, capped them, and then laid them back down on the marbled counter top.

One to three minutes I needed to wait, both boxes had instructed.

I moved to sit on the bathtub's edge and tapped my toes on the tiled floor as I waited, in a trance, my own breathing loud and too close. And then, without meaning to, in my peripheral vision I saw four pink lines appear on the tiny plastic screens of the tests. Two pink lines on Clearblue, two pink lines on First Response.

I stared at the four pink lines. And then I stood up, screamed, and threw the empty boxes of two pregnancy tests against the wall. My eyes focused on the tests that still lay on the counter top. My fury turned toward them, and they too were flung through the air. I fled to my bedroom.

The rest of that morning, I lay still like a corpse, drunk on pain, inebriated by despair. Hours ticked by, and I could feel the sun moving through the sky. I had not studied enough; I had done nothing. I considered calling the university and pleading my case to someone.

"Fuck that. Fuck!" I half-whispered, half-screamed. I tore some lined paper out of a notebook and slammed the microeconomics textbook down on the kitchen table.

I had approximately six hours to study. The exam was at six thirty and I could sail in at six twenty-nine, everything fresh in my mind, word-vomit on the exam booklet, and parachute right back out.

Anger was an incredible centering tool. *This must be how monks feel when they focus on one solitary thing and all else fades to nothing*, I thought. I studied in a state of delirium, devouring pages of the textbook, skimming through the chapters, writing down the important bits and pieces. The anger was rooted in a pool of fear, and this pool fed the roots as they grew into rage.

I collected all my handwritten notes in a fistful and took them to campus.

I sat in the parking lot, the sun casting its waning golden hues all throughout my car. I read over each page of notes twice.

I wrote the exam.

I marched back out to my car, the cool April evening taking its place quietly, lightly. I wanted to lay my head on the steering wheel like some cartoon character. Instead I turned on my phone.

Two vibrations: text messages. The temporary bubble popped. The outside world was still there, still existing and moving forward in time even while I was momentarily being swept underwater. The inevitability of real life came into view as two notifications on my phone; one from my best friend, one from my boyfriend.

Roslin said that her period cramps made her want to rip out her uterus, Jesse was telling me that he saw four deer that morning.

Breathe in and breathe out. Now again, and again, and again.

The sun had long faded by the time I arrived home and dissolved into the couch.

I didn't open Jesse's text. Smoking, drinking, unbothered Jesse. Jesse leaning his head over the edge of the truck bed, looking up at the round moon, and taking another pull from the joint that rested between his index and middle fingers. Jesse, the terrible gift wrapper, who had recently learned to overcome this by simply dropping everything into a gift bag and crunching up tissue paper to put on top. Jesse, the boy who ran his pinky finger through the condensation on the bathroom mirror in a heart-shape, I saw it after getting out of the shower.

Jesse, a pending father to be.

I didn't want to disrupt his world with *my* problem.

I had never been scared of Jesse before, but I was then. A chasm had split the ground between him and I.

I struggled to heave my upper body off of the couch, twisting my hips to let my legs fall over the couch's edge, and in doing so, feeling the ache of the six cuts on my upper thigh.

Fuck, I whispered.

I touched my hand to my thigh. I should have cut deeper. Maybe if I damaged my body enough, the fetus would realize this was not a safe home and move on.

VIII

The newfound pregnancy seeped through my brain like an oil spill through a body of water. My mind rejected the entire concept as water rejected oil, but the oil spill persisted and contaminated every good thing.

Life marched on at precisely the same pace it had always marched at. I had another counselling appointment coming up. And increasingly worried, then frustrated, texts from Jesse kept coming.

It did not feel like a fetus inside of me, it felt like a deadly pathogen I had contracted.

At seventeen, I had faced myself in the mirror, and had sworn on everything in heaven and on Earth that I would *never* bring a life into this world. I could not live with myself if that life inherited the mental health issues that I had. I could not bear for that life to resent me silently as I resented my own parents for bringing me into existence. Therefore, I had not once contemplated pregnancy and was deeply convicted in my soul that I would not have children. I had always naturally gravitated away from babies and young children anyway.

Even though life was heavy with fog, the lunacy of humanity tells one that they know what lies before their feet. But then the next foot put forward does not stop going down, and suddenly you're free falling through cold mist, shrieking.

That was where I found myself: in the free fall, a limp body falling hundreds of feet through blankets of fog, with no view of the cavern floor.

I went for a long walk the next morning. Nature had now undressed entirely from its winter clothing and was trying on new spring apparel. Tiny emerald green leaves were beginning to uncurl out of their bud-homes. Orange-bellied robins were retrieving tufts of grass and beak-fulls of twigs for nest building. The grass was beginning to recover from its despondency in winter. I did not bring earbuds with me, I walked in silence. The strengthening rays of sun easily filtered through the still bare tree limbs.

I walked and walked, sometimes in pensive thought, and other times lulled into a rhythm of mechanical movements alone.

Take a breath, kid, I told myself, using Jesse's vernacular. I smiled. I liked being called *kid*. I had not spoken to Jesse in two days and reading through his multitude of texts, he was on the verge of calling me on the phone. The last thing I wanted.

I had options, Dr. Allis had said. She had said this matter-of-factly, in gauged and measured words and in a tone smooth as honey falling on toast. She had professionally told me I could get an abortion. The word fell heavy in the room as she said it. Transparent, invisible weight.

Abortion.

Label that as wrong, they had said. I said, *okay,* and did so. That was the extent of the story thus far. But thus far I had not been pregnant.

I went to a small coffee shop a few blocks from my apartment. I brought a book so I could put on the facade that I was there to read and sip black coffee. I wasn't interested in either, I simply needed to be outside of my four walls and around other human beings who were moving down the linear tract of their own lives as well. I needed to be out of the atmosphere of my own place, where it was just me and my thoughts that could get so dark they blacked out the world, like two blinders on a horse.

I felt a small movement in my purse resting on my hip as I walked to the coffee shop. It was my phone vibrating. I didn't have to look to know it was Jesse calling. I let the phone ring in the dark cavern of the purse.

I ordered an Americano from a barista who looked so young for having all the tattoos she had. As I watched her pull a shot of espresso, I tried to discreetly look at her tattoos: the swallows, the lavender, the poem, the wishbone, the knives, the peach.

The girl smiled and handed me a tall lemon-coloured mug of piping hot coffee. I sat in the corner of the shop, the farthest away from the front door. I needed to think about what I was going to say to Jesse. As the coffee hit my bloodstream, my stream of consciousness gained speed.

Thoughts of a sterile clinic, a covert abortion operation, a secret kept, a single memory to lock away and repress until it was only a myth. But I could not go far along this pathway of thought before running into the wall that was either fear or my conscience—I often could not tell one from the other. I hit that wall like a trapped moth banging into glass. A transparent force field, thin but impenetrable.

The Americano was cooling. I took the book out of my cloth bag, set it beside my coffee, and opened it to a random page. I rested my cheek on my hand, eyes down, pretending to read. I didn't bring a single word on those pages into focus.

I couldn't contemplate abortion without a choking fear and self-loathing. I knew where my parents stood, I knew what they told me.

Anyway. I crushed up that train of thinking like an aluminium pop can and threw it as far away from me as I could.

Did I need Jesse's blessing before getting an abortion?

I picked up my phone and sat, still and silent. The soft indie soundtrack lilted throughout the coffee shop. Jesse's multitude of text messages lay before me in my hands.

Finally, I typed out, *Can I call you in a few hours?*

In less than two minutes Jesse texted back, *3 your time? When I'm on lunch.*

Sure.

The last sips of the Americano were cold, and its thick, silty dregs coated my mouth in bitterness. I put the book back into the bag without having read a single word.

I walked past a sleek row of shop windows and saw my little frame walking along beside me. My shoulders arched slightly forward, torso pushed backward, subconsciously hiding the sesame seed fetus. I had looked more pregnant after the dinner rolls and cherry trifle of a Christmas dinner.

The faces of my parents kept breaking into my thoughts. I knew their principles; therefore, I knew their verdict: have the baby, live with the consequences, abortion is murder, and we would rather our child not be a murderer.

The afternoon inched forward, and my skin was sticky with sweat.

I almost threw my phone across the room on instinct when it started to ring and Jesse's name appeared on the screen. In my planned version of events, I would be the one to call Jesse, which would somehow give me the driver's seat for the conversation.

I debated not answering at all and texting, *sorry, something came up, call you later!* But I found myself answering after the fifth ring.

"Hey."

"Hi," the velvet voice that did not match the unrefined boy bled into my ears.

"Hi," I said dumbly.

"Long time no talk."

I detected annoyance, which instantly quickened my heartbeat.

"I know," I said. "I'm sorry."

"It's okay." He sighed. "I've just been worried is all."

"I know, it's just been … a little busy and—" I fiddled with the hem of my shirt "—Yeah, just a little busy here."

"You're almost done with university now, yeah?"

I didn't know that Jesse was keeping track of my schedule. Christmas presents in January and birthday wishes in the later afternoon of my birth date were the norm for him. I wasn't particularly bothered by those two things.

"Heading into the final week of exams." I forced a smile into my voice. I knew it would translate over the phone. "I'm almost done."

"The stress is almost over for you."

A pause, longer than what could be considered comfortable, ran between us. Being pregnant was an abhorrent secret I aimed to wrestle down myself, suppress it until it surrendered, suffocate it until it died. Telling Jesse this secret was not adhering to those rules of play. I gritted my teeth and pushed the words out of my mouth: "Jesse, I'm sorry I've been silent, but I've had a lot on my mind. I have to tell you something. You deserve to know— actually, I want you to know that you're the first person I've told and—"

"Okay, just say it."

"Alright, just—" I couldn't bear to contend with a raised voice. My emotions had never been so fragile. "I had blood tests done recently. And they found out that I'm pregnant."

It was irrevocable now. My head collapsed into my hand and my eyes closed. The world narrowed like a spotlight shining onto a stage, but the light found only me.

Jesse's voice brought me back from the numbed-out state I had projected myself into. "This is my baby?"

"Of course it's your baby."

"And they're sure?"

"Yes."

"The results can't be faulty?"

"I took two tests at home after they said the blood results showed a pregnancy." The four blush-pink lines were scars in my memory. "Both pregnancy tests were positive as well."

I heard male voices from Jesse's end; he said, *hold on*, a few more distant voices, Jesse's breathing close to my ear, and then a door closing.

Silence. Then a vexed sigh.

"Kid. I don't know what to say, honestly. I'm just—I'm at a loss. I don't know what to say right now."

"I know," I nodded, though he couldn't see me. "I know. I'm not entirely sure what I expect you to say either, if that helps."

"It doesn't."

I shifted uncomfortably. Jesse was upset in that painfully cold manner that chilled me to the bone.

Finally I said, "It doesn't make sense. We always use condoms. Did you get cheapo ones?"

An empty sigh. "No, I didn't, Imogen. We had sex, like what, six times—"

"Five times," I corrected.

"—Five times."

Two detectives, spending time on a futile case that had already closed.

"Well," I said finally. "What are we going to do about this?"

"About this pregnancy?"

"Yes. About … it."

"The baby. You can say *baby*, Imogen."

"Well, it's a fetus."

"Oh, fuck being politically correct."

I blinked. "I wasn't trying to be politically correct. Just more biologically accurate, is all."

"Honestly, Imogen, I can't have that conversation right now."

I bit my lip and wanted to scream. I didn't want to have the conversation either. "Well, okay. Are you going to call me back later?"

"Yes." Dead air. "Of course."

We didn't say *I love you* to each other, we just ended the call simultaneously.

I was glad to be off the phone with Jesse, but then I was back on my own iceberg again.

Like, what, six times? repeated in my mind in his voice. It had sounded credulous and careless. Or was that just how I had heard it?

Sensitivity: a key critique of my sex. When animals sensed minute changes in their interactions, it was lauded and labelled as higher intelligence, that kind of cunning perception. But not so in the human species.

My fingers paused in uncertainty as they took up their daily task of picking up a glass of water in one hand and a small orange clonazepam pill in the other. This was not *advisable*.

Dr. Allis had not made this issue sound urgent, but suddenly, there were implications for me looking after my own health.

I swallowed the pill along with a small dosage of unwanted guilt that felt funny and unfamiliar. I needed to make an appointment with Dr. Allis. But what would the sense be in that if I was just as lost as I was the last time I was in her office? Maybe I could force myself to make a decision under a self-imposed time frame.

There was still no word from Jesse, only an automated email reminder from Sonya telling me that I had an appointment with her the next day.

I fully intended to keep quiet about the growing poppy seed inside me. I had only told Jesse because I felt obliged to.

One last exam was staring me down with indifferent eyes.

Miyu was once again corralling the girls together for an evening of studying. It would be the last one. Hannah, Salomé, and Miriam were there. Hannah's honey hair was silky liquid on her back, swaying along with her every movement. Miriam and Salomé were seated at the yard-sale kitchen table. I sat down, too.

Miyu informed us that Salomé had written her last exam earlier that morning. I politely clapped along with the girls and swore under my breath. This would not be a productive study time.

Miyu spoke like a queen. Stories effortlessly folded in on one another. She was the leader; everyone else fell behind her, no matter the assortment of individuals surrounding her.

The studying accomplished was minimal, at times hardly detectable. Miyu got good grades regardless of what she did—

blessed golden child. But her life could not have been without sadness, I would tell myself. Her parents had divorced years ago, and that was when her mother had packed up Miyu and her brother, leaving their home in Japan for Canada.

The condition of Hannah's grades was not clear. Mine were stable but certainly needed hours of studying to maintain.

The natural instinct of every university student set in, and Miriam offered drinks: a bottle of already opened Pinot Grigio, canned cider, gin and tonic—but no lemons or limes in the house. Salomé said cider, Hannah said Pinot Grigio, Miriam's eyes slipped over to me, and I said, *same.*

The next minute, I had a generous glass of white wine placed in my hand. My stomach felt like liquid magma, scalding and seething, when I saw the alcohol and remembered. I set the wine glass down on the table and pretended to concentrate on my notes.

The sun was taking its leave and the house was dimming. Miriam got up and turned on several light switches. The kitchen was set ablaze with artificial light that refracted into the ageing glass of wine.

I smiled and laughed when the girls smiled and laughed, though it was too loud in my head to know what it was about.

After a time, Miyu's gaze fell to the wineglass, and I intercepted. "My stomach is feeling a bit off," I said. "Nerves I think." I sighed delicately. "The exams."

The girls' faces fell in concern. Miriam said I could lay down, Hannah offered Gravol medicine she kept in her purse. I said that maybe I needed to go home early and rest.

"I'm sorry the wine went to waste," I said in a tone that could be interpreted equally as jest and sincerity.

"Oh," said Miriam. "No, no, don't worry about that. No big deal. We'll drink it."

I gave a small wave to Salomé, Hannah, Miriam, and Miyu and slipped out the door.

I took the little orange tablet of clonazepam the next morning too. Again, guilt. I had never felt self-conscious or guilty about taking medication before. And now it was just one more weight added to my conscience.

Jesse wasn't calling or texting me. As the length of silence grew, so did my anxiety. I was the messenger and he might shoot me.

The days were getting longer. April was caving in on itself, each day another leaf awakening, another sunbeam strengthening, another wave crashing against the shores of time. Something was changing and growing everyday inside of me as well. The earth and I travelled parallel lines.

The sun was slowing down and beginning to take its sweet time to sink into the horizon. I was able to take my daily walks and jogs later and later in the day.

I sat quietly in my car as another sunset bloomed, its light reflecting off the rear-view mirror and nearly blinding me. Liquid gold coated everything the evening light touched as the shadows grew taller.

I stepped out from behind the wheel and faced the sun, feeling its dying light. How lovely that we could live on a planet whose sun set the way ours did. The gilded light made my skin look smooth and tanned as I walked toward the door where Sonya's office lay directly on the other side.

The familiar couch awaited, a new box of Kleenex patterned in a gaudy design sat in front on the coffee table. Forest bumped her head as she clambered from underneath the table to greet me. I petted her where she had bumped her head and then sat down.

Sonya began. "How have you been feeling since our last appointment?"

I had been pregnant the last time I had sat on the couch. But I had not known.

"I've been alright," I said as the laugh track of a sitcom played somewhere in the background of my mind.

"How would you rate your mood on a scale of one to ten?"

I decided to tell her that I was feeling like a four.

Sonya continued through her usual list of questions. I answered them as if I were still living in the week before. It was shattering to think that all my life I had been marching toward these weeks without knowing. Trajectory is set before everyone. I was not special.

Sonya asked me if I was taking my clonazepam daily. That was the first question I nearly tripped over in answering.

I didn't know how soon pregnant women needed to get their lives in order so they could biologically grow a healthy baby. Dr. Allis hadn't told me to get off clonazepam immediately, or else a baby with some loose wires would come out in eight months. Nevertheless, my mind had latched on to her words and had contorted and reconfigured them in every way imaginable.

Sonya asked me about Jesse and my heart felt like it had dropped fifteen stories.

Sonya wasn't blind. She observed first the stony line of my mouth that hardly budged when I spoke, then my eyes that became glassy with despondency.

Sonya asked me to name one thing I could see, one thing I could smell, one thing I could hear, and one thing I could touch. This was a grounding technique she had prescribed to me whenever I spoke about the wiles of overwhelming anxiety.

"I see a blue jay in the tree outside," I said as I gazed out a towering window. "I smell something sweet, like something was baked in the kitchen."

Sonya nodded knowingly but did not divulge what had been baking in her kitchen.

"I hear Forest breathing. And I feel the warm air from the vent underneath this couch on the back of my legs."

"Good," said Sonya. "Very good. Now breathe in." Sonya lifted her hand upward, palm facing the sky, tracing the subtle rise in her own chest as she modelled the exercise.

"Now let that breath go," her hand fell gently back into her lap.

My breath released, far too fast, like a sigh.

"How are we feeling?" Sonya asked.

"Hm." My eyes fixed on nothing, though they were pointed at the cream-white wall behind Sonya. I opened my mouth but no words came. I closed my mouth and kept looking at nothing. A small burning in the throat that signalled the building of tears began. Flames licked up my esophagus.

If I spoke, my voice would surely crack like glass.

Sonya waited, and Forest remained utterly unbothered until the dam broke and tears dripped off my chin and cheeks onto my lap. It was then that Forest abruptly lifted her head and tilted her head ever so slightly to the side, almond eyes the colour of burnt sugar questioning me. *Why are you crying, Imogen?*

Of course Forest couldn't speak, but Sonya could, and so she asked for the both of them, "Can you tell me what's upsetting you?"

Open-ended questions, always. The bread and butter of therapy.

My tears continued to run, and they continued to wait. The silence between us was growing in length and weight. I had to say something. Sonya would wait a year until I said something.

"I found out something this week."

"What did you find out?"

I shrugged.

"Good news or bad news?"

"It's subjective."

"Was it good news or bad news for you?"

"Bad," I said. "Very bad."

"Are you comfortable telling me what this news is?"

I shook my head.

"That's fine. Have you talked to anyone about this?"

"Yes."

"Did you feel supported and understood?"

I thought of Jesse in B.C. I thought of Jesse running through a forest, a make-believe vision of him I had created long ago. He is running on a misty morning, the forest floor slightly damp. Jesse's head is light and free, rabbits dart out of his way, a black bear sees him from afar and laughs to itself, belly full of Saskatoon berries. He is at peace.

Forest was lowering her head back down to its resting place. She had lost interest.

"I feel ... heard, I guess. I told them. They needed to know, so I told them."

"If they needed to know, then it's good you told them," Sonya said. "Are you feeling any better after telling them?"

I lifted my right shoulder slightly in a shrug that could mean either yes or no.

"Is there anything more you'd like to tell me about this?"

"No, I'm good," I said, as if a waiter had asked me if I would like my water glass topped off.

The session passed the halfway mark, and I was keenly aware that I kept steering the conversation away from Jesse whenever it got too close to him. His name was a red-hot metal coil on the stove that would burn my mouth if I spoke it.

From Sonya's standpoint, she must have assumed I had found out Jesse had cheated on me, or perhaps I had cheated on him.

We continued to volley the conversation back and forth between patient and counsellor. It all felt stupid and pointless; there was nothing meaningful in it for me. My eyes had dulled and I wanted to sleep.

Sonya wanted to book another appointment while I was still there. Often, she offered to book the next appointment either at the end of the hour or she would say to give her a call. Evidently Sonya felt something was not right, and she wanted the appointment made before I was outside her four walls. I said yes to the first date she suggested and was ready to hightail it back to the car.

Forest arose from her dog bed and padded over to me as I tied my running shoe laces into bows. Her wet black nose pushed into my cheek, her way of saying goodbye. I ran my thumb over the silky hollow of snout and forehead that all dogs have between their eyes and mouthed *bye, Forest*.

A cool evening breeze swished into the room as I opened the door to leave. The sunset was long gone, leaving a dark, onyx sky. No stars glittered above. Even the moon was hidden away.

A grip of icy anxiety, colder than the breeze, pulled at me. I knew that a severe panic attack awaited me just around the corner, perhaps in my car, perhaps not until I got home. Regardless, the aching trepidation was in my bones. The outside felt dangerous, while the glowing yellow warmth of the room at my back felt safe.

This sentiment had occurred in my thoughts before: *let me live here, let me be here.* I would find a safe person, a safe atmosphere, and I would want to stay. I would imagine that I could take shelter in a person or a place, and there would be something to stand between me and the darkness that I spent so much energy day after day fighting off.

I had paused too long in the doorway and needed to walk forward in order to avoid an odd situation, yet the bottoms of my shoes cemented to the floor. I felt the sensation of a dream state, when the air is dense and murky, and one cannot move forward, try as they might.

This is absurd, I thought, getting frustrated with myself.

"Is there anything else?" I heard Sonya's voice float through the air behind me.

"No, sorry," I cast a smile behind me, my gaze nowhere near meeting hers as she looked on after me. "See you later."

I clicked the door shut behind me and scuttled to my car.

Silence fell. A few cars and their headlights glinted through the trees in the distance, Sonya's long laneway separating me from them.

The familiar rushing of panic sounded throughout my heart and mind, and like a sailor watching dark royal blue and grey storm clouds roll in, I was alert to every signal of danger. I bent my head to the side and rested my cheek on the inside of my arm holding the steering wheel.

Tight chest, shallow breathing, dimmed vision, unfounded fears, racing thoughts.

I found myself back at Sonya's door, knocking gently at first, and then with more urgency. Only one lamp seemed to still be lit in her office. Maybe she wasn't even hearing me.

Waves of panic kept churning, closer and with more fury.

A gold-orange light flickered on in the hallway, then another light, and then finally the main office light.

I felt like a mentally ill lunatic. Despised myself for it.

Sonya reappeared, her soft skin creased, though I detected something in her expression that told me she wasn't surprised. Maybe I was not the first client to immediately come back after an appointment. Maybe others had rushed back to her door.

Sonya didn't say anything but held the door wide, allowing me to step over the threshold and past her.

"I'm not ..." My throat burned with words. "—I don't ..." My esophagus constricted as if it were collapsing in on itself. "—I don't know what to do right now." One tear slipped out, and I felt it gently roll down my cheek, leaving behind enough of itself for there to be nothing left by the time it reached my chin.

"Come, sit." Sonya motioned me to take my place back on the couch.

My throat kept burning. I swallowed again and again, trying to get the lump to dissolve.

Finally, Sonya spoke, "Can you tell me what you are unsure of?"

My head was down, eyes fastened on my long fingers, pink nail beds, and white crescent moons that lined the bottom of each nail. For a long time, I studied my hands intently until the vision of them began to rapidly blur and their outlines pooled together. My eyelashes became wet and stuck together.

"I'm pregnant. The blood tests show that I'm pregnant."

"Are you having a panic attack right now, Imogen?" Sonya asked.

I couldn't see my hands anymore, but I sensed that they were shaking, and that's what Sonya must have noticed.

I said yes.

Fear had the minimal decency to only dissolve, into the brain, one or two fears at a time. Panic attacks were twenty or thirty fears imploding in the mind. Psychological repression set in immediately after the panic subsided. The fear turned otherworldly and obscure like a dream you couldn't remember as soon as you woke up.

Through a haze, I heard Sonya asking me to breathe in and out, in and out.

Forest came into the room next, the secondary counsellor, padding in with an uncertain look, an invisible bubble-letter question mark floating above her coal-black head. Clients didn't often come back and dissolve on the couch in hysteria. She was unsure what was happening.

My stomach had turned into a pit of snakes. Slimy, alive.

The baby would be gifted fifty percent of my DNA. This horrified me. It should never happen. I could end the pregnancy in secret and live with a rotting heart and accusing conscience. I could silently beg for my parents' understanding every time I stepped foot in their home.

By then, Sonya had gotten my breathing down to a reasonable rhythm. Oxygen in, carbon dioxide out.

My gaze stayed nailed to the floor, my head heavy like sand.

The spectacle had concluded, and I felt like a deflated balloon.

"Can you breathe better now?" asked Sonya.

"Yes," I said. "Mostly."

My pregnancy had been stated, and now it was on the table to be discussed.

"What would you like to talk about?" Sonya asked.

Sonya had no thick notepad in her hands this time. She must have set it down and not retrieved it for this impromptu counselling encore. Forest, on the other hand, had assumed the regular position, snout resting between two paws, at ease beneath the coffee table beside Sonya's chair.

"I got the blood tests done," I finally said. "To see if there were any issues there, like we had talked about."

There had been one notable issue.

"I went for a follow-up appointment, and that's when they told me. They said I was pregnant."

Still floating on the surface of an entire ocean of denial, I let an unbelieving tone seep into my voice.

"How do you feel about that?"

I lifted my hand out of my lap and vaguely waved it in the air, in the general direction of life. I thought it was obvious.

"I had a panic attack in the doctor's office, and then I went home and slept." I left out the glass, the blood, the garbage can full of crimson-splotched Kleenex and paper towels.

"I'm very sorry to hear that."

"Yeah." I shrugged. "It's been hard."

I was shutting down then. I had said what I said and was tired and it was up to her to pull at the ball of yarn until something gave and I unravelled into transparency.

I pulled at one of the pillows that sat on the opposite end of the couch and hugged it to my chest. No need to maintain a sense of dignity any longer. I had shattered all sense of self-aggrandized propriety when I knocked at Sonya's door for the second time in one day.

"I never imagined this would happen," I said quietly. "It's unthinkable."

"Unplanned pregnancies can be difficult. The last thing you need to do is feel as though you are alone. You said you had told someone?"

"Only Jesse."

"Only Jesse. And what was Jesse's reaction?"

I shrugged. "Stunned. Overwhelmed, probably. I'm not even sure."

"Was his overall reaction positive or negative?" Sonya began her pulling at the tangled mess of thoughts and emotions.

"Negative. But Jesse doesn't really get that emotional about anything. He was just ..." I trailed off for a few seconds before finding my way back to the sentence. "He was just Jesse about it."

Sonya nodded slowly but made no effort to speak.

My phone conversation with Jesse had left me on a sort of cliff-hanger, no real verdict given by the father. I had been swimming in the anxiety of not knowing what Jesse was thinking or feeling for days now. Would he pressure me to end the pregnancy? Or would he demand for me to grow his child in my body?

Jesse, *head of a household.* The thought sparked hilarity. Men, the heads of households, the first to run. The trope of absentee fathers.

"I don't think Jesse wants to be a father right now," I said. "I haven't heard from him since then."

"And what about you? Do you want to be a mother?"

"No, I don't want to be a mother. Not ever. It's not just that I don't want to be a mother *now.*"

"I understand," Sonya said softly. "Do you have a plan for moving forward?"

"I have no idea what I'm going to do. There's no plan." I pinned my hand down to my thigh with my other hand to stop its shaking, and felt the biting ache of healing flesh wounds beneath. "It's almost like I am too tired to even think about this. Dealing with my own self is enough."

"I understand. And it is fine to feel that way and good that you are identifying those feelings. Let's think about where you were nearly two years ago."

Two years ago I had been in a psych ward, my mind a poisonous cavern that had nearly killed me. The lean doctor that tended to me looked stretched thin, like plastic losing its colour as it's pulled apart. He looked in need of the empty hospital bed beside me. Little dark moon crescents rested below his eyes as he told me that I was lucky to still be alive with no lasting damage to my heart. I then lied my way out of the hospital, wanting the earliest release date possible. I was nowhere near stable.

"How do you think you might have handled an unexpected pregnancy two years ago?" Sonya asked.

"I couldn't have." I would have gone straight home, only after taking a minor detour to the liquor store to purchase whatever held the highest alcohol content. Once home, the alcohol would help to wash down every pill I came across in my search until I collapsed in a heap.

"So," Sonya continued. "You're here right now; that's part of handling it. You are able to handle this now."

The past week had felt like anything but *handling it.*

I had Googled *abortion* and read countless articles. I felt isolated. Everyone already knew which side of the battle line they stood on. I walked on the fence, terrified to come down on either side.

"But I don't feel like I'm able to handle it."

"Feelings can be deceptive," Sonya said. "You are alive, you are here, you are making a healthy choice by seeking help. No one could ask more of you than that. You're going to be okay. You really are."

My face felt numb, my legs did not feel even remotely attached to my core. I was some intangible entity gazing down on the room, on my chestnut hair, wet eyelashes, mascara-streaked cheeks, and shaking hands.

"I don't know how to go forward. And every day that passes without me making a decision, the thing inside of me keeps growing." I bit my lip.

"Remember to breathe, Imogen. Slow down."

"But it feels like a time bomb ticking down. Either I detonate it and people will hate me for it, or I throw myself on top of the bomb and I die myself."

Sonya steepled her fingers. "Can I stop you there?"

I paused.

'What do you mean by that?"

"I mean—" I swallowed and my throat ached from its tightness. "—That either I have an abortion and some people will hate me for it, or I have the baby and I just … die inside, I guess. It is inconceivable that I could handle having a baby with my mental health the way it is right now."

"You believe some people will judge you if you have an abortion?"

"Yes. And some people hate women who have abortions."

"Who would hate you if you had an abortion?"

I looked past Sonya's shoulder to gaze out the window, into the black void of night. "I'm not sure," I said.

"Would your close friends hate you?"

"I don't think so."

"Who else could hate you?"

"My parents."

"Do you really believe that?"

"I'm not sure." No. They were not capable of hating their child. They would not hate. Beloved daughter, yes, always beloved, and yet a grandchild killer, miracle-of-life-ender. Irreversible damage, something very deep down, near the core of what bonded parent and child, would erode and turn to dust.

"Sometimes we can only rely on our own moral compass, Imogen. We have to know our own heart and the motivations behind our actions, even if people looking on cannot, or will not, learn what those are. Sometimes—" Sonya steepled her fingers and rested her chin on the peak. "I'm just trying to think about how I should word this" —her eye contact broke away, and she looked pensively at something immaterial. The old grandfather clock that housed Time, *tick ticked*. "Do you think that it is possible for an action to be neither right nor wrong, but neutral?"

Tick, tick.

Sonya lightly pushed three fingers against her chest. "Our heart, our motivation, and our circumstances are important. These three things are *very* important. I am aware that you were not raised to believe along that line of reasoning because it appears to devalue moral living. Makes things wishy washy, right? From what I know of your childhood, you describe a— well—a sort of exacting moral code. Would that be fair to say? Please correct me if I'm wrong."

Nodding, I said, "That's quite fair."

Sonya stayed quiet for a moment. "What do you think your parents had in mind when they instilled a moral code of conduct into their child?"

I stalled and pretended to think.

"Or maybe, to put it another way, what is the function of moral values?"

"To ... get us to function morally?"

Briefly Sonya acknowledged the play on words with her burnt umber brown eyes. "I would agree with you. Yes, I think that the purpose of a moral code is to produce moral living. That's straight forward enough. And so, I would like to ask, do you think that it is possible for a moral code, or a strict list of rules, to produce moral living for every possible scenario under the sun? For every variable?

From the cadence of Sonya's voice, I knew she wasn't demanding a response, and so the question hung there like a cloud that had gotten lost and had floated in through the window.

Sonya smiled. "This was not meant to turn into a philosophy session, I'm sorry. Please stop me if you feel that what I am saying will not be helpful to you. Alright?"

She paused then. Now looking for a response.

"Alright," I said.

"Would you like me to continue?"

I nodded, yes.

"It seems, to me personally, that a strict list of rules actually *cannot* achieve its purpose. With an infinite possibility of motivations and circumstances, strict rules cannot generate moral living for those variables. Frankly, I think we as humans intrinsically know this. Let's say ..." Sonya tapped her fingers on her knee. "Let's say a child's pet dog is running toward them. Now let's say the child's parent picks up a rifle and shoots and kills the dog. That's horrible, isn't it? It would be terrible to kill a child's pet, much less kill the dog right in front of them. In that scenario, that is a bad parent."

Sonya continued. "Now, let's look at a different scenario: a child's pet dog is running toward the child. The dog has rabies. The child's parent picks up a rifle, shoots, and kills the dog. Now that is a good parent. In both scenarios, the choices and actions of the parent are the exact same, but one parent is bad while another is good. That scenario may have been a little morbid, but I know you will understand the meaning. The actions are the same in both cases, and yet they are different because heart, motivation, and circumstances are important variables. We could sit here and come up with an endless number of scenarios. So many that eventually we would come to the scenario of abortion. Right? And we could think of many variables for the scenario of abortion. You're aware of some of them already. For this scenario, I would say that you are by far the most aware of the variables." Sonya leaned forward in her chair. "You are most aware of the variables, Imogen. Of course, we have to acknowledge the conversation surrounding this particular scenario of abortion. And that is *who*. *Who* makes the decision about the variables. And I know you are well aware of this conversation."

We shared the briefest bittersweet smile.

"And I'm not here to tell you what decision to make." Sonya leaned back into her chair again. "I only want to help you feel that you have the freedom to decide."

"It's really hard for me to think that way," I said after a while.

"And that's alright." Sonya nodded reassuringly. "I want to leave you with this: an invitation to momentarily think outside of the parameters you've been given. You don't need to throw them out or divorce yourself from the principles you were raised with. But I invite you to simply step away from them for a moment. You are free to go back to them if you choose. Only, try to step out of this situation for a moment and think about how you would care for a girl in the same circumstances you are in. How would you speak to her? Are you able to help this girl make a decision when fear and anxiety do not hold sway? Does this make sense?"

I shook my head up and down cautiously. I understood what Sonya was saying, but the invitation felt impossible to accept.

Sonya offered me a glass of water, which I declined. She asked me if I felt I might experience another panic attack, I said no. I understood that it was time for me to go. I wondered if Sonya would charge for this extra time and tack it onto the bill that always graced my inbox shortly after an appointment. I never paid while I was at Sonya's. She didn't like being paid by a client when they were still under her roof, she had said at the end of the very first appointment. It felt like a direct transaction, she had said, for the help she offered. She preferred an honour-like system. I could have dined and dashed after the first counselling session if I had wanted to. Maybe it was another form of trust building that Sonya implemented or another psychological game played by a shrink. I had always harboured a suspicion of trickery in the field of psychology. Not so much with Sonya though, she really didn't seem the type.

I left and wiped the mascara off my cheeks.

I was a poor nighttime driver and missed one of my turns. But I did not turn around, only kept going, further and further down the city street. I saw the glowing yellow arches and pulled into a McDonald's drive thru. Being a creature of strict habit, it was so rare for me to drive down unknown roads or unexpectedly buy fast food. But due to recent events, I had lost some of my grip on the reality I once had. The rope had slipped a few inches through my fingers. Nothing felt real anymore, so why not have a large fries to go.

I checked my phone as my car idled behind the vehicle in front of me, as paper bags of chemicals and additives were being passed through the window, as tall cups of sugar water followed.

Still nothing from Jesse. I felt alarmingly close to becoming a statistic: unplanned pregnancy, runaway father, single parent. Epitome of cliché.

I ordered a large fries and a Diet Coke. By the time I got back to my apartment, I had eaten all the fries and was sipping on the last of the fizzy soda that popped and sparkled in my mouth. The outside light automatically flicked on as it sensed my movement in the driveway. It was nearly ten o'clock and all the warmth that the April daylight had offered was now sapped out of the air completely. I looked up into the night sky, black as hell, darkness that covered lightyears. I exhaled deeply and my breath plumed upwards in a cloud and then vanished into the atmosphere.

Before even opening my door, my mind was already roaming all over my apartment. It landed on the shard of glass that I had once again placed at the back of the kitchen cupboards.

I struggled to pull those thoughts up out of the dark like a sailor pulling up an anchor from the depths of the sea.

I opened my laptop and looked up the size of a five-week-old fetus. A sesame seed. The fetus would be the size of a sesame seed that gets stuck in your teeth and only comes out with floss. The father of this sesame seed remained silent. A flash of anger zipped through my chest. *Fuck you if you think you can detach from this,* I thought. I stewed in silence for several moments, before my anger landed on a solution: if Jesse did not contact me within the next week, then I would detach him from having any right in deciding what we would do about the pregnancy. Forget *we.* There would be no *we* if he didn't accept joint responsibility.

I picked up the book that I had started reading weeks ago. My heart stuttered and then stopped briefly as I thought about my past self who had put the bookmark into place. She was gone now and at the time I had not known that she was merely days away from never existing again; there was no goodbye or closure, just the ash and smoke of where she had been.

IX

I moved through the subsequent days in purgatory, neither here nor there. Neither pregnant and having a baby, nor pregnant and scheduling an abortion. Jesse was neither absent nor present. Still not a peep from him.

There was a murkiness to those days, an uncertainty. I brooded; I had panic attacks. I waited. I waited on Jesse, but I also waited on myself. I was waiting on myself to find a path. The next week had come, and I had told myself that I would revoke any right Jesse had as the biological father of the now slightly larger sesame seed under my flesh. I had been momentarily scared off the internet after I had landed on a site that led me from an article comparing the size of a fetus to various seeds, nuts, and fruits, to a subsequent article with rules about feeding and changing baby diapers. I wanted to stop reading so badly but didn't. Several articles later I slammed my laptop shut.

On Friday: a text from Jesse.
Sorry for taking so long to get back to you, the message read.
'Get back to you', as if we were playing phone tag.

It's been a lot to think about. I think we should talk on the phone again. Soon. When can you talk?

Jesse's ghosts were scattered all around the apartment and yet it seemed nearly impossible to imagine him standing anywhere near me. Everything felt out of place, nothing felt real, the sunshine cast unfamiliar patterns in my house. This new world was colder.

And another change: I spent a long time thinking through the wording, the tone of texts before sending them to Jesse. Now eggshells stretched as far as the eye could see and I was scared to say something that would push him to a distant place.

And so I sent no words to Jesse for several hours, which then turned into half a day.

I took a shower at three in the afternoon. The cocoon of warmth disintegrated as soon as I stepped back out onto the bathmat. My apartment was one of the many homes on that particular line of latitude which, in the early days of May, sat with neither heat nor air conditioning. There was always a period in the spring and in the fall when we lived naturally in tune with the temperature of the earth.

I sat on the edge of my bed, phone in hand, naked but for the bath towel that was loosely wrapped around me. The towel carefully covered my stomach. Subconsciously, I had begun averting my eyes from the soft flesh of my stomach.

I had to tell Jesse something; I would not cloak myself in silence as he had done.

Finally I lightly typed out, *I agree. I think we should talk on the phone soon,* and shivered violently at the thought. And then one more message: *I can do a phone call this evening. Whenever you get off of work is fine.*

Okay, came Jesse's instant reply. I wanted to toss my phone into a fire at the phenomenon of Jesse being on the other side, at that exact moment, being that closely connected for one moment.

Victoria startled me with her small cat-chirp and jumped into my lap. Her almond-shaped green eyes reflected the lamplight.

"I wish I only had to take care of you," I whispered, just a few inches above her triangle ears.

Dinner was a bowl of canned soup and one large carrot, cut up into sticks. I realized that neither Jesse nor I had actually stated who would call who that evening. Unease settled from six o'clock onwards. I needed to know things like that ahead of time.

I distracted myself with the washing of dishes, watering the plants (apologizing to some of them for the neglect), and refilling the bathroom's soap dispenser.

It was Jesse who called; I had waited him out.

"Hello?"

"Hi." Jesse's voice. Close and familiar. "How are you?"

I almost said *I'm good* without even thinking. But no, this was Jesse. I could be a little more honest than that, couldn't I?

My eyes roamed the ceiling. "I guess I'm surviving," I said.

"Yeah," said Jesse.

There was a beat of silence, and I curled my toes instinctively in discomfort.

"So," I said. "How are you?"

I could hear the rustling of blankets. He must have been lying on his bed after his day of work. "I've been better," he said.

"Me too. Anyway, how was work?"

"Work was fine. Tiring. I have to be honest, Imogen, I don't really want any small talk right now."

When he used my name like that, it was like drinking ice cold water when one was already cold. It only made me colder.

"I didn't know that was small talk," I said reflexively. "Just asking my boyfriend how work was."

A sigh. "I'm sorry. You know what I mean. Don't you?"

"Yeah." I did.

"How are you feeling? Physically, I mean. Any morning sickness yet? Or is it too soon for that? I have no idea when pregnant women get that. I actually know nothing about pregnancy."

"Me neither. And I was never planning on learning about it either. But anyway, to answer your question, no, I haven't felt anything physically to indicate that I'm pregnant."

"Goddamn. It's insane to hear you say that."

"That I'm pregnant?"

"Yeah."

"I think I've said it enough times in my mind now that I don't immediately want to throw up when I say it."

"Have you told anyone else?" asked Jesse.

"I have. Just my counsellor."

"Your counsellor?"

"I have a new counsellor. Her name is Sonya."

"I don't remember you telling me about her."

"Maybe I haven't," I said. I believed that, in Jesse's mind, counselling was only a psychological game that involved paying someone with three or four framed degrees on their wall to listen to you.

"How long have you been going to her?"

"About three months now, I guess." Time flies when it's measured in the frequency of shrink sessions.

"Is it helping?"

"Yes." It felt good to acknowledge out loud. "It is."

"That's good. I'm glad."

"Hm," I breathed. "Me too."

I thought about Jesse lying on his bed. I thought about being there, tucked in the crook of his arm. I thought about how that scenario would never play out without a new sharpness inserting itself into the softness of two young people being in each other's arms. I should have held him tighter the last time, branded the image of morning sun bathing his chest and arms and white sheets in my mind. But it's difficult to know what you don't know.

"Hey, I was really anxious when you weren't talking for so long," the words slipped out of my mouth. I hadn't meant to say that.

"I had a lot to think about," Jesse said.

"I know. I did too. I just meant … that was hard on my anxiety."

"I don't really know what isn't hard on your anxiety, Imogen."

"I'm just asking for some kind of acknowledgement that the situation wasn't handled well." I needed an *I'm sorry*. Pointless though it may be if you had to ask for one.

"I don't know what to tell you. I was busy with work and I had to think about this whole thing."

I wasn't going to get what I wanted from Jesse, and his emotional fragility could not boil into anger right before delving into a conversation about the pregnancy, and so I abandoned that trail of conversation.

"Okay," I said slowly. "I need to know what you are thinking."

"Do you want me to be tactful or do you want me to be blunt?"

Jesse occasionally surprised me by the art of his dialogue. It was rare, but sometimes I caught glimpses of his deeper being. It was intriguing, a flickering light on the horizon.

"I guess you might as well just be blunt." My anxiety had already given me a full rundown of every worst-case scenario possible, so what was the worst he could say to me?

"I can't be a father right now," Jesse said. "I don't think I have any right over your decision about whether you can be a mother right now, but I know for certain that I can't be a father."

My heart cracked.

"So, what are you saying?" I asked.

"I'm not going to tell you whether or not you should get an abortion."

"Okay."

"But what I am telling you is that I cannot be a father right now."

I closed my eyes and touched my fingertips to my temple. "You're saying that I can either get an abortion and life will go on, we can go on, or I keep the baby and lose you."

"That's a harsher way of putting it, but … fair, I guess."

"Did I word it incorrectly?"

"No. That is essentially what I'm saying."

Blood began to seep out of the cracks snaking through my heart. And along with the blood, hope. I had known that the unplanned pregnancy put my relationship with Jesse in jeopardy to some extent. The three-year relationship was entering a red danger zone, I had known that. I just hadn't known how it would actually feel. But I knew then how it felt: another falling, nothing beneath my feet.

Where do I turn? I thought. *Where is help?* The ever-present safety net of my parents was not beneath me. They could not sympathize—not this time.

Three years given up on?

"This is tough, for sure," Jesse said with a casualty that ignited fire in me, "—but you're smart. I'm sure things will work out."

Things will *work out?* I wanted to scream and laugh hysterically.

"It feels like we aren't making this decision as a team," I said.

"What do you mean?"

"I mean that we are not both bearing equal responsibility in deciding how to move forward. Like—" I began to struggle with breathing. "—You've made your decision on your own already. We haven't talked about this together at all yet. We haven't tried to solve this together."

"What?"

"I feel abandoned, Jesse."

"I'm just telling you where I'm at. I'm being honest with you."

"Alright. Thank you for being honest with me. But you've made a decision independently. You've jumped off and abandoned ship without me. We either abandon ship together or we stay on board together." What was I even saying? It was the only metaphor I was able to grasp and put forth.

"So, you want me to lie and say sure, I'll be a dad?" Jesse's voice was gaining the characteristics of a knife's edge.

"No. You misunderstand what I'm saying. We haven't made a decision about this pregnancy together. There hasn't been a conversation."

"I don't know what you mean, to be honest." Jesse was minutes, maybe seconds away from shutting down and cutting off all access to his emotions. I felt like the conversation was already over, and somehow, I was about to be declared the loser.

"I just told you where I'm at and how I'm feeling," Jesse finished.

"And that's fine, that's valid. That's good you told me. But now you're leaving the decision in my court."

"Yeah. And you have the freedom to make up your mind one way or the other."

"But it's not just us. It's you, me, and … potentially some other entity."

He half-laughed. "The baby?"

"Maybe baby, yes. Perhaps a fetus."

"Imogen, grow up and call it a baby. You don't have to walk on eggshells, no one is listening to this conversation."

"That's not what I was getting at. I honestly don't know exactly what to call it. I don't know at what point, biologically or ethically or whatever, it's a baby and not a fetus. What I was saying is that you're abandoning me to either single-handedly save the pregnancy or not."

Silence.

"Do you know that some people would criticize me for questioning the difference between a fetus and a baby, and others would criticize me for even feeling the need to worry about a difference? Like, my parents couldn't even conceive of—"

"I think you are blowing this out of proportion," Jesse interrupted. "You do this all the time. Calm down."

"I'm not—" I stopped my fury. "I'm trying to tell you why I'm feeling like I am."

"You don't have to think so broadly or worry about so many things. It's just you, and you can make whatever choice you want to."

"I realize that is what you think"—*holy fuck*— "but I'm just explaining to you why it is not that straightforward for me."

"Okay, well, I know you think a lot. And you'll probably need a millennium to think this over, too."

"Actually, this kind of thing has a pretty limited amount of time."

"You still have a lot of time to think. It's a personal choice you'll have to make."

"I am not sure how to explain this to you, but it's more convoluted than that."

"But who would even know that you had an abortion if you did get one?" Jesse asked in frustration.

"Well, my parents, for one," I said.

"And how would they find out?"

"I would … tell them?"

"Why?"

"Because I couldn't live with that kind of secret. I couldn't be in their house with that heavy of a secret. That would be unthinkable, really."

"Everything is out of proportion with you," said Jesse. "Girls get abortions. Girls keep babies."

I thought about the fact that if I kept the baby, I would need to change medications. I wasn't sure what seven or eight months without clonazepam would mean.

Crimson heat was creeping up my neck. "My doctor said that I would need to change my medication if I keep the baby. Clonazepam is not recommended for pregnant women, and clonazepam is the first medication I have found that has worked well for me with few side effects. Do you know how devastating it is to hear that I would need to go off of it?"

Jesse sighed. "That sucks, I'm sorry. At least it would be for only nine months."

"That's true. But a lot can happen in nine months, and everything could just … spiral." My memory clawed back in the annals of my medication history. I could not remember all the odd names of the medications I had been on throughout my life, but there had been many. Some had all the effects of a placebo pill. Some increased suicidal thoughts tenfold.

"A lot can happen in nine months, you're right."

"I am very scared, Jesse. And now I feel as though you're on the brink of abandoning me. So, I guess I'm even more scared now."

"Look, don't think of it that way. I'm not abandoning you, I'm just giving you a choice."

"But you're not—we're not—making the decision about the pregnancy together. Do you not get that? Am I not explaining myself clearly enough?"

"Am *I* not making myself clear? I cannot have a baby right now. You can if you want to, I'm not trying to sway you one way or the other."

I rubbed my eyes.

"I don't know what else to tell you or what more I can say, Imogen."

We were fast approaching an impasse; Jesse was shutting down.

"Okay," I said slowly. "I feel that this conversation did not go well and that maybe we should both cool down and have another phone call later. Maybe tomorrow."

"I don't need to cool down. I've said what I said. I don't have anything more to say."

Deep breaths, kid, just breathe. Another small piece of my heart fragmented as I referred to myself by the nickname Jesse had given me. He had not used that nickname for me once in the conversation.

"Alright, well," I said. "I, at least, feel that this conversation has not gone well and would like to talk again about this later."

"It would just be a rehashing of this conversation, so what's the point?" said Jesse. "I really don't feel like talking this through again."

I wanted to crumple up like one of the paper dress-up dolls my grandma used to give me. Put me away, in a musty darkened drawer, and take me out again to play a different character. I knew I was not meant for this world. I was meant to be a bird, moss on a stone, seaweed on the ocean floor.

"Imogen," I heard Jesse shifting over pillows, sheets, the comforter his mom gave him for Christmas. "I seriously doubt that any good will come out of another conversation. You know what I think now. You're going to have to calm down and think this through yourself."

"Jesse, wait. Can you promise me something?"

"Sure."

"Can you promise me that after this phone call, maybe tomorrow and over the weekend, you will think about what this is like for me? What this means for me? Please just put yourself in my shoes and think about this from my perspective."

A slip of silence.

"Okay, Imogen, I will. I need to hang up now though," said Jesse.

I moved my head, relatively in agreement. "I guess I should be going to bed now anyway."

"That's true. It's nearly eleven there. Far past your bedtime."

I half expected Jesse to tack on *kid* to the end of that sentence. But he did not. It was his phrase to lighten every conversation. *"Don't let me down, kid. Wherefore art thou, kid? Don't worry so much about that, kid."*

I yawned. "Well … goodnight."

"Goodnight."

"I guess we'll talk later? Sometime?" The cavern kept splitting. The ground beneath us was suddenly shooting toward the sky, under each of our separate footings until we would be on the peaks of two separate mountain tops.

I wanted to leave. Leave the human body and go for a long, long walk into the woods, deep into the heart of a forest, or maybe a dry and arid place with sandy soil and a flat horizon.

"Yes," Jesse said. "We'll talk later."

"Okay. Have a good sleep."

"Thank you, you too."

"Thanks. Goodnight."

"Goodnight."

Jesse hung up first, and I slowly lowered the phone away from my ear.

It would have been nice to cry, but my tear ducts were depleted. I had never cried so many times in such a condensed period of time, and my body had apparently not thought ahead to prepare a surplus of tears. So instead, I simply ached that deeply profound ache that drives one straight into the fetal position. It was that ache that lies heavy in the chest and resonates in the bones.

Before crawling beneath the Mennonite-made quilts, I wrote in the next day's small square on the wall calendar: *Make appointment with Dr. Allis.*

As I lay in bed, I pictured all three hundred and sixty-five squares on the calendar lined up, end to end. An infinite of squares.

I dutifully called the doctor's office the next day and wrote down the date of the appointment.

Not much can be said for the four days following. One day I had to stop in the middle of making a split pea soup, the knife I was using was toying too much with my mind. Every slice of onion and celery made me think just how easy it was to slice away at flesh. Granola and grapes were eaten for dinner instead.

Another day I woke up and felt my stomach as cold sweat clung to my forehead and temples. At five thirty in the morning, I flipped on the blinding bedroom light and ripped off my shirt to stare at my stomach in the mirror. Yes, it did appear to be extended ever so slightly. I turned off the light and ran back to bed. By the end of that day, I decided that I must have been bloated. My stomach once again appeared to be back to normal. But my mind was playing tricks on me and my OCD became solely focused on the shape of my stomach. Every time I went to the washroom, I pulled up my shirt, turned sideways, and gazed in rapt trepidation at my reflection. Sometimes I was sure my stomach was beginning to swell like bread dough, and other times I was convinced that I looked exactly the same as I had before. I went back and forth between the two, sometimes within the same hour. My eyes couldn't be trusted to clearly see what the mirror reflected.

Another cold silence ensued between Jesse and I.

All conversation ceased after the phone call. It seemed to be the unspoken rule that we would not speak again until I decided what I was going to do. I made up conversations in my mind; I imagined that I was speaking calmly to Jesse, making him understand that we were still together, we could still be a team. In other make-believe conversations, I was throwing a plate past his head to signify that he was being a useless shell of a person.

I drove back to the medical clinic one sunny afternoon for my appointment with Dr. Allis. I parked my car at the farthest edge of the cracked parking lot, far away from where I had parked the last time. That parking space was cursed. I did not come early to the appointment this time. After compulsively reading articles here and there about pregnancy, I realized that if this situation were to continue, I would be visiting the doctor quite a lot, and I did not need to spend extra hours of my life waiting in a parking lot.

My attention was naturally drawn to another pregnant woman who sat in the waiting room. Her black hair sculpted her face like a frame and two russet brown eyes peered at a *Chatelaine* magazine. I considered picking up a magazine myself but opted for gazing at the blue and yellow fish that meandered around the fish tank. I watched a fish bury itself in pebbles while another nibbled at some speck that was gently falling to the bottom of the tank. My gaze was drawn back to the woman, where it fell to the floor beneath her feet.

After several minutes, the pregnant woman looked up briefly and we caught each other's eye. Reflexively I smiled politely and the woman smiled too, before we both instantly resumed our muses. The smile slid off my face when a man entered the large waiting room and walked directly toward the woman. She kept her head bent over the magazine on her lap. My anxiety suddenly spiked like a sugar rush and I wanted to warn her.

The man's leather boot-clad feet must have come into her field of vision, and the woman looked up, her silky pin-straight hair moving with her uplifting face, like a curtain parting.

She smiled and said something to the man that I couldn't hear. It was her partner.

My gaze trailed after the couple as they left in a haze of stability.

"Imogen?" A voice sang out over the heads of everyone in the waiting room.

I almost sang back, *here!* as I had in elementary school when class attendance was taken.

I turned and it was the same nurse as before. A thin, tall woman who slumped slightly, as if she disliked her own height. The nurse led me to precisely the same hospital room as before and I sat down in the same seat as before. It was an unsettling déjà vu.

I was the knocked-up girl who was going to doctor's appointments alone, ordering takeout for one, baking cookies and freezing half the dough.

The nurse had my medical records at her fingertips and she knew, even if my stomach was as flat as the first time I had walked into the clinic. And my doctor knew and Jesse knew and Sonya knew. The secret was slipping through my hands like water.

My Roslin didn't even know, and I told her everything. Everything anyone had ever said to me under the context of confidentiality was told to Roslin. Our vault of secrets was one and the same.

The nurse asked the usual questions, half-heartedly, since she had just seen me. How much worse could one be after seven days?

"Medications are the same?" The nurse asked.

"Yes," I said.

"No changes to the dosages?"

"No."

And then I was left alone to wait for Dr. Allis.

I looked at the sink and instantly saw the salty tears *plop plop* to the scratched metal bottom in my memory.

Dr. Allis was taking her sweet time.

I studied the fire escape plan that was posted on the wall and nearly screamed when Dr. Allis entered the office. I had been completely absorbed in my daydreaming.

"Good afternoon, Imogen," Dr. Allis said. "How are you?"

I nodded. "I'm fine, how are you?"

"I'm doing well," She sat down, smiled, and adjusted her silver pen to align perfectly with the edge of the counter top. "Now, where were we?" She studied my file for a moment.

"Oh yes, yes, I have some things for you." Dr. Allis slid her rolling chair to the side, opened a drawer, and pulled out a small stack of pamphlets and brochures held together with a red elastic band.

I knew what they were before she even handed them to me: information from a local pregnancy centre, a whirlwind overview of the first three months crammed onto a single easy-to-read pamphlet, and a *Your First Pregnancy* leaflet printed on blinding happy-yellow paper.

I took the stack of paper from Dr. Allis's outstretched hand and set the brochures on my knee where they balanced precariously.

"Now there's a lot of information there, but don't get overwhelmed," explained Dr. Allis. "The most important piece of information would be this here." She tapped on the edge of a pink and purple brochure for the women's pregnancy centre that sat on the top of the pile. "They can help you a lot with any questions you have about pregnancy, your options, etcetera. And last time I had mentioned the issue with the medication ...?" Dr. Allis's cool blue eyes looked up briefly and then snapped back to her hand, poised to write something medical down.

"Oh, yeah," I said.

"So, I mentioned that we do not recommend pregnant mothers take clonazepam. I think we should look back at the medications you have already been on and see if you think one could work."

I wasn't looking, but I imagined Dr. Allis's eyes trailing down the list of medications I had been put on and then taken off of during my teenage years. Teenagers were experimenting with illicit drugs, while I was experimenting with my own cocktails of prescription drugs—far less fun, I would imagine.

"Was there any medication that you have taken in the past that you felt helped you?" asked Dr. Allis.

"No," I said.

Sometimes the benefits could not justify the side effects. And sometimes there was no benefit. Clonazepam had been the elixir my body responded to. Clonazepam told my brain to shape up and it stabilized a brain that was turning septic.

I shrugged. "Clonazepam is really the only medication that helped me that much."

"Mm," The doctor now tapped the pen on her chin. "I'm a little hesitant to put you on a new medication altogether since we really don't know what side effects you may experience. But, that being said ..." She sighed. "We can't have your mental health deteriorating for the next eight months. If you choose to keep the baby that is," she added quickly.

I nodded in agreement.

"There really is no medication that has helped you other than clonazepam?" Dr. Allis began reading off the list of medications that I had been prescribed throughout my teen years.

One of the names she read was certainly not an option, as I had taken up cutting my skin in earnest a mere week after starting the medication. The oblong flaming red pills had heightened my suicidal tendencies tenfold, and I ended up calling my mother, who had been buying butternut squash and tomatoes at the store, in a panic.

"I think you need to come home, Mom."

"Right now?"

"Yes, right now."

"What's wrong?"

"I really want to kill myself."

"I'm coming right this minute."

"I think it's the new medication."

"I'm coming right away. Stay on the phone."

And that had been the end of those pills. The other medications had never been lethal like those ones, only insignificant oddities from there on out.

My eyes closed as I tried to recall specific details about each of the multi-syllable names.

I tried to picture what each pill looked like. One had been a beautiful turquoise-green, but I couldn't remember what name on the list to match the image to.

After the red pills came the Forgotten Years: ages sixteen to eighteen. I don't know what happened during that span of time, only that I sometimes barricaded my bedroom door and didn't leave my room, spent days on end in the dark with the curtains pulled shut, and wore the same clothes too many days in a row. The few medications that I had been on during those years were unmemorable.

"Do you remember how you felt on any of these medications?" Dr. Allis asked.

"No, not really," I replied. "I guess ... Seroquel wasn't too bad." I tapped my fingers nervously on my thigh.

"Alright," said Dr. Allis, picking up the file. "You didn't experience any severe side effects from Seroquel?"

"I don't think so." If the side effects had been too bad, then surely I would have remembered. Yet if the medication had helped, then surely I would have stayed on it.

"I can write you a prescription, and you can get it filled whenever you ... or if you need it. Does that seem alright?"

"That seems alright."

The sound of scribbling on paper.

I took the prescription the doctor handed to me.

We finished the appointment off with niceties. Was there anything else I should tell a medical professional? Hemorrhaging of the spirit? Sleepless nights? Heart strings severing?

I withdrew into my thoughts, finally saying while holding up the brochures, "I will look over this information."

"Please call and make an appointment if you need me; otherwise, we should have a prenatal appointment once a month for the first twenty-eight weeks, unless the pregnancy is terminated."

"Good to know, thank you."

We smiled goodbye, and I saw it in Dr. Allis's face: the soft cheeks strained, mouth not effortlessly able to smile, as if to say, *God help that baby if it's carried to term.*

The stack of brochures and pamphlets instantly found themselves in the kitchen Drawer of Nothings. The Drawer of Nothings contained the extra buttons that came attached to the insides of new sweaters, bits and pieces of small hardware that Victoria found, and pens that had nearly run out of ink. That was the drawer where the brochures ended up.

Another run was needed; old Nikes, uneven braids, leggings worn thin between the thighs, a white tee shirt.

Days were slipping through my fingertips and, being propelled forward against my will, I was forced to open the Drawer of Nothings and revisit the stack of brochures. Some of the pamphlets were shades of hyper-femininity and motherhood, rose pink, mauve, and magenta. I read those pamphlets last. Some of the pamphlets referred to *you and your partner*, others did not, and I preferred the ones that did not. By process of elimination, I landed on a professional looking green and white pamphlet, the contact information printed on the bottom.

My fingers pressed the sequence of numbers into my phone, and I held it up to my ear in uncertainty.

An impossibly young-sounding voice answered the phone, and I thought that perhaps this was a co-op placement for a student of social work. Lots of experience to be had at a pregnancy centre.

I stumbled across a few words before telling the girl that I was interested in making an appointment.

Their next available appointment was not until the next week, and she reiterated that if this was any kind of medical emergency, I should point myself in the direction of the nearest hospital and start walking.

I told her that no, this wasn't an emergency, and that yes, I would like to book their next available opening.

When the phone call ended, I had an appointment marked on my calendar: *1:30pm at PC* (pregnancy centre).

I shoved all the brochures back into the Drawer of Nothings.

Just keep going, I told myself.

Into what future? I asked myself.

Not sure, I replied. *But you must keep going.*

Why?

I don't know.

Anxious thoughts flitted manically in circles like trapped moths. I had no idea where my feet were heading, but I was moving forward through time. Everything unknown.

X

The appointment date glowered in the distance, its yellow-orange eyes becoming brighter. And then it came.

They gave me a long questionnaire at the pregnancy centre. The questions were straightforward and I answered them absent-mindedly until they began asking about the beginning of my pregnancy, about the conception. Since conception was the spark that burned the forest down, I avoided thinking about it.

Did I know the date of conception? No, not the precise date. But I did know the start and end dates of the possible time of conception. And, to be more precise, I knew the five times that Jesse and I had had sex.

Although Jesse had said six? My gaze trailed away from the questionnaire. I didn't know why he had said that. God knows he must have kept track of the number of times we had intercourse since I was sure he had been hoping for a much higher number.

I decided to write down the date of when Jesse and I had first had sex (roughly twenty minutes after I had arrived at his home) and then a dash followed by the date of the last time we had sex.

And maybe the last time ever. I instantly recoiled and my heart drained of blood. *Maybe that was the last time I would ever have sex with Jesse.*

I completed all the forms and set the pen down.

The lady who ushered me into her office was the opposite of Dr. Allis. Unkempt, wiry grey hair was pulled back by a headband made to suit the taste of a twelve-year-old. Her skin looked tired, her whole figure looked tired. She must have been in her late fifties. All the pregnant women in crisis had tired her out. The office itself looked new, everything washed in white. The L-shaped desk was littered with the woman's family portraits and porcelain figurines.

"Imogen." The lady peered at a piece of paper that must have had information about me on it. "Imogen Waterhouse," she repeated, pronouncing my first name incorrectly.

"Yes, that's me," I said.

"Good, good, we have the right person," she chuckled and took off the glasses she had used to read my name.

I nodded meekly, looking around the office full of medical diagrams of uteruses and nine-month road maps to pregnancy.

"Imogen—I've always liked that name, Imogen—my name is Elise."

The window of time I had to correct the pronunciation of my name had closed.

Elise launched into an introduction of the clinic and how they could help me. She questioned herself once or twice and had to look up information from the centre's website. Spans of silence ensued as she searched for answers. My eyes wandered around the office, the pristine newness suffocating slowly from the posters and office supplies.

Elise tucked a chunk of peppered hair behind her ear and it immediately sprung loose. Her children pictured in the array of photographs on the desk had evidently inherited her thick, unruly hair.

"Own Your Magic" was etched into a fake stone that sat beneath her computer screen. I felt uneasy. Perhaps the pink and purple pamphlets would have been alright after all.

"So," continued Elise.

I folded my hands tightly in my lap. I chided myself, yet I could not help it: I concluded that Elise was, in one word, a *dud*.

Elise pulled out various sheets of paper, some pastel and pretty, and all littered with information I was meant to read and comprehend. Next, Elise brought out a couple of sturdy pamphlets, ones I could refer to repeatedly. There was a lot of paperwork everywhere. Many trees had been cut down for this.

Elise leaned over the desk and circled different bits of important information.

"Do you have a fridge?" She asked.

"I do."

"We have a magnet!" Elise produced a large magnet with the pregnancy centre's logo, their hours of business, phone numbers to contact, and one inspirational quote.

Elise kept going, words falling on words like a waterfall. I crossed and uncrossed my legs as I tried to play the role of pregnant mother.

Nothing was intrinsically wrong with Elise, but I felt I was being asked to entrust her with my life, or at least this part of my life, and I simply did not trust those hands with their yellowing fingernails.

I left the pregnancy centre feeling depleted, a star collapsing in on itself.

My eyes played tricks on me every day as I obsessively checked the profile of my stomach in every mirror—even at a Walmart once, the bathroom empty and the fluorescent lights humming. The day would come when there would be no mistaking it: I would start to show and I couldn't blame the meal I had just had, or the amount of water I had just drank, or the bloating I believed I might have. There would come a day of reckoning.

My connection to Jesse was a fraying rope. Bits of brown fibre wore thin and then broke. There had been no communication.

On the other hand, Roslin was notably not silent and let it be known that I had been quiet and aloof. I scrolled through my texts to her over the past few weeks. She was right; my texts were vague and dull like automated responses, no beating heart behind them. I didn't keep anything from Roslin, and I realized how much heavier things were to carry alone without her.

My parents were wondering if I had a job yet for the summer. In every text, there was veiled concern about my finances and work situation. Didn't I know that it was *May*?

I knew. The fetus was like a reversed IV drip, leeching the vitality from my bloodstream.

I tied on my Nikes and went for a long walk. The sky was filled with wisps of clouds that looked like they had been pulled from cotton balls.

I wanted to put everything down, my head and my heart, put the baby in someone else's body, and leave. I had tried putting two of those things away for good before and was firmly told that I could not by the nurses in the psych ward. Sleep was the only form of mild escape.

In the waking hours, I began to think about the number in my bank account. The number was decreasing and I had calculated when it would go into the red: late summer or early fall, just before the leaves went red. One of the papers from Elise was an infographic with cute clipart like a children's book. Thrift stores were your best friend, it said, if you were on a budget. I threw this piece of paper away from where I laid in bed, and it fluttered to the floor like a leaf. I wasn't stupid enough to think that I could work over the summer. Being out of bed was work.

I continued to lay on my side, despondent, eyes occasionally moving from the wall to the paper on the floor.

I was not at my parents' country home and there was no water to run to. I was landlocked. I had always found the crashing of waves to be inexplicably calming. Jade-blue coloured water, white crest on repeat, ever on repeat.

My parents lived near the water, I had grown up by the water, and so the lake was a friend. But there was no water here.

I found a bottle of guava-orange juice at the back of the fridge, not yet expired. I sipped on it and pulled open the Drawer of Nothings. The pamphlets lay in a heap as I had left them. I pulled one out, then another, and another, until half the kitchen counter was covered in paper. I needed forward motion, my claws scratched for traction in time, and so I read each pamphlet. Carefully, discerningly. There was no time for another Elise. I called a different centre and made an appointment and wrote the date down on my calendar. Five days away and more time would pass by.

Five days passed. This pregnancy centre was in a little suburb that hugged the east edge of the city. The building was older and a little plaque on the wall said it was founded in 1981. The inside of this centre was almost entirely white as well, but tired, the wood of the desks scratched, many of the posters aged from sunlight.

The woman who ushered me into her office wore a name tag. *Emma-Rose*. She had a softness about her; soft eyes, soft smile, soft, deep voice. Emma-Rose told me that the centre could help me in every stage of pregnancy. They had doctors and nurses, and the doctors could perform abortions.

"Right here?" I asked in surprise. "You do abortions right here?"

"We do, yes," replied Emma-Rose.

I had always pictured an abortion taking place at the end of a long, dark and winding hospital corridor.

Emma-Rose's hair was shoulder length and orange like carrot juice, freckles graced her cheekbones and nose, and gold earrings peeked through her tresses.

The tired walls that stood around us had seen my story so many times before, they were probably bored of it. Being pregnant did not feel quite so alien in that room. I wasn't special, I didn't stand out. My spine pushed gently into the back of the chair as I watched the human lick of light in front of me chatter about Braxton Hicks contractions, postpartum depression, and the neonatal period.

Three weeks later I was standing by the lakeside. Finally, water. It was June and the previous days of rain had culminated into a roiling, frothing body of water that swallowed up more of the shoreline than usual. It was a mild day, but by the water it was cooler. I set my gaze on the horizon, and even though it looked flat I knew the waves coiled and crashed upon one another all the way out there too. I was at the edge of the shore, the waves rushing up to greet me and then receding in shyness. I had stood on that lakeside so many times before.

As a toddler, I toddled along this shore. As a young girl, I had waded out until the water lapped around my flat chest, the small rocks in the sand jamming my toes into awkward positions. As a teenager, I had come here in the winter time when no other soul roamed over the large mountains of frozen snow and ice. When I was twenty-two, Jesse and I had built a campfire on the beach and fashioned a cocoon for ourselves with an old blanket.

I sought solace in this water and it had always brought me some amount of peace. I thought perhaps it could comfort me again. A strand of hair blew around my face and stuck to my lip. I lifted my hand, brushed it away, and briefly rested my hand on my stomach before letting it fall back down to my side.

Now I was twenty-four and pregnant, toes touching the edge of one of the Great Lakes, and the father of the baby was absent.

Bits and pieces of driftwood had washed up on the sand and a few logs had been pulled around to suit the needs of visitors. I found one and sat down.

I had seen Sonya just the week before. I sheepishly walked through her door for the first time since my breakdown and delicately placed myself on the couch.

Always one for being cagey around the subject of suicide with my past counsellors and therapists, I maintained aloofness around the subject, feigned surprise when the word was spoken. I did not tell her that death lived just on the other side of my front door, knocking, knocking, knocking, driving me mad, waiting for me to kindly open the door.

My obsessive thoughts had fixated themselves on the slip of prescription paper that lay in the Drawer of Nothings. I reasoned that if my future self decided to keep the baby, then I should quit the clonazepam. Pre-emptive action. I could still end the pregnancy, filling the prescription didn't mean anything.

I stood up and walked back toward the water's edge. I bent down and slipped my fingertips past the surface of the green-blue lake. The water was still cool, carrying the memory of winter. I crossed my arms over my stomach and began to trudge through the sand back to my car.

I will fill the prescription as soon as I get back to the city. I will, I will.

It was the warmest day of the year thus far, the day that I filled the prescription at the pharmacy. The sun was hot but still too far away from our hemisphere to burn skin or singe grass. Like when reaching for something just centimetres away from one's grasp, so the sun was stretching out to reach us but coming up shy. I savoured those days before the summer came in all its sultry fury.

The pharmacist said that the prescription would be ready in fifteen minutes. There wasn't anything of interest near the pharmacy to walk to, save a pet store located in the same strip mall. I had been there multiple times before to hold squirming guinea pig bodies and the lime green snakes that curled around my arm. I didn't want to be the lunatic who kept showing up to handle the animals and so I stayed put. I wandered down the aisles until I was in the makeup section. A million packages for the same kinds of black, brown, and blonde sludge. The nail polish selection had always been my favourite since I was only tall enough to gaze at the first few shelves. The dark crimsons and flaming reds had seemed so womanly and bold; the movie women used that colour. My younger self could not wait to snatch up those tiny glass bottles when I was old enough. I would keep my nails red and perfect. Everything I held would be wreathed by those almonds of red.

As I had lightly padded around the earth, mud brown hair braided by my mother, I had thought there was so much wisdom and control to be had in adulthood. Somewhere between the realm of the Roman gods—Luna, Sol, Hercules—and my child-brain was adulthood. I would know so much; I would do so much.

I looked at the shades of lilac and light pink on the pharmacy shelves. I did not paint my nails red. It was too gaudy and loud for my plain body.

The pharmacist handed me a little white paper bag that I tucked into my purse. I tore through the metal staple that held the bag closed as soon as I got home and held the plastic bottle up to the light like it was an illicit drug. Pale yellow. I had not taken the orange clonazepam tablets for days, having become scared of the most helpful medication I'd known. Scared to be bad and take care of myself.

I took out one of the yellow pills and washed it down with a glass of water. It would take several weeks to settle into my system. I could not remember how Seroquel had affected me before, and with trepidation I once again acknowledged that if Seroquel had helped then I would have stayed on it. I tried to not think of that and set the new pills down alongside the clonazepam bottle.

Victoria was fast asleep at the foot end of my bed, but I needed to hold her for comfort.

I picked her up, her whiskers were bent out of shape on the side of her face that had been pressed against the bed.

I held her close to my chest and felt a purr stutter and start like an engine. Victoria had been a scared kitten, trembling limbs and paws, ready to retreat to the deepest, darkest corner of the house at the slightest sign of danger. I cooed and coddled her like a baby until she was no longer the trembling mess of nerves. And after I had been there for her, she was there for me. After therapy appointments and psychiatrist visits, Victoria was waiting at home, happy to curl up against my tired body.

Jesse and I had not spoken for many weeks. Our relationship was in another dimension. It existed, yet it was not tangible, a dispersing fog, contingent on the fetus inside of me.

Little fruit cups filled the refrigerator shelves, the only food I wanted to eat most days, and several blankets and pillows billowed outward from the couch like a soft underwater sea creature. TV series and movies began to run together like paint, creating a singular mass of monochromatic abstraction. Things looked easy enough for Rachel Green—blonde hair framing her face, options for father figures, a laugh track in the background.

It wasn't until I had two panic attacks in one day that I realized I had been there before. I had walked in a six-year circle and was back at the mental state of my eighteen-year-old self, debilitated, the body I lived in hell-bent on driving me out. Black and purple spots projected onto the wall in front of me as I lay disorientated and suffocating under too many blankets. I had been in bed since dinner time the day before. Then I heard the mail lady bang close the metal mailbox affixed outside the front door and knew it had to be after one in the afternoon the next day. I threw the pillow across the room that had been wedged for hours between my stomach and knees. I arose, turned, and threw my fist into the wall. I heard my knuckles bang sharply into the drywall, no damage to the wall.

I had been frustrated all day. Frustrated with myself. Why was everything so hard? Why was I so fucking sad all of the time? Why did it take everything within myself, all my concentration and energy, to get out of bed, braid my hair, peel an orange? Why did I feel like a pseudo adult, trying to keep up with the race, but my legs were far shorter than everyone else's?

I was disintegrating just as I was told to be at my peak in order to grow a baby and give birth. Growing a life was killing me. My heart was beating at a lazier rhythm since it believed it wouldn't be asked to pump blood for much longer.

I was struck with another horrifying thought in the middle of a Saturday: what if I were to have the baby, deteriorate mentally until I could barely hold a spoon, and *then* kill myself? Become a mother who had the audacity to leave their child alone and abandoned? Become as negligent as a father?

I half-heartedly browsed job openings for several hours, applying to a couple positions that seemed straightforward enough for someone like me with administration experience. Maybe I needed to be *distracted,* as they say. I always failed to see how simply being distracted could solve much.

Victoria stretched and yawned in the slanted light of a sun that had decided to peek out through the clouds in the late afternoon. Bless the little dullard, she lived in a haze of oblivion. I looked through the living room window and decided it was already too late in the day to go for a walk. My eyes caught on the lilac bush in a neighbour's front yard. Little purple buds were just beginning to open into the four-petalled flowers. The air around the bush would soon smell like perfume.

Anxiety crawled under my skin and curled its spidery legs around my heart.

My stomach curled in agony and bile rose in my throat. I ran to the bathroom and heaved up several mouthfuls of vomit into the toilet. I watched the water in the toilet bowl dilute the vomit and then swirl it away.

I felt the clonazepam being squeezed out of my brain like a sponge. The Seroquel was decidedly not holding down the fort. With clonazepam I was often able to walk myself through situations and scenarios in my mind and decide which option would result in the best outcome. Now safety barriers were crumbling down and waves of fear were eroding what had once held them at bay.

The house of my mind was on the seashore and I watched in horror and trepidation as the tides inched closer to my front door every day. What would be the condition of my house at the end of a pregnancy? Where would the waterline be after another six months? Up to my chin or above my head?

I stepped into the kitchen. The refrigerator whirred and I breathed in and out.

I fixed a small breakfast of cut up apples and a bowl of oatmeal with a zig zag of honey on top. I sat down at the table for two. I decided I would be okay that day. I would be alright, I would survive. No need to think about the days to come, I need only think about the day I was existing in.

I cleared breakfast and let the empty bowl streaked with gooey oatmeal sludge soak in warm water. I called Sonya and made an appointment, I called the pregnancy centre and made an appointment. I smoothed down Victoria's fur that was sticking out haphazardly after she had bathed herself.

"You're a little braindead," I told Victoria. "But I like you just the same." She curled up into a little doughnut shape and fell asleep.

I heard my phone buzzing with a call. I was similar to a criminal on the run; people were trying to track me down. My mother, occasionally my father, and Roslin. I was the Artful Dodger of aloof avoidance. I could say just enough without saying anything at all. And it never hurt to have a reputation of peculiarity to take cover under when needed. Being normal seemed an exhausting facade to maintain and cater to. I declined the call.

XI

It was while I was getting into the car to drive to Sonya's the next week that I noticed it: the little convex curve of my stomach.

I felt everything within me sink into the grave. And I died. Finally, all of my hallucinations, analysis, and mirror checks were no longer mirages: it was there.

My eyes were drawn to my hands and they seemed detached from my body.

Fuck, fuck.

A panic attack slithered toward me.

My eyes burned red and itchy and I blinked furiously.

Three months ago Jesse had been in the province, and I, in his arms.

I clenched my hands around the steering wheel in two vice grips and ground my teeth together. I wanted to scream and cry and tear down the sky. How many more times could I stave off suicide? I wasn't sure. But I did it, again and again, somehow.

The tiny Hello Kitty pendant on the key chain tinkled and swung around as I turned corners too quickly. Jesse had given the pendant to me during our first Christmas as a couple. God only knows what possessed him to buy it. We had not been dating long and found ourselves in that murky time of relational uncertainty (to buy a gift or to not buy a gift). In hindsight, we had not known each other well. After our first year of dating, when Jesse and I had been driving down a dirt road in the backwaters, the keychain clinking furiously with each unceremonious jostle of the car, I finally asked Jesse, "Can you tell me what went through your head when you purchased this keychain?"

Jesse had laughed sheepishly and shrugged. "Girls like Hello Kitty?"

The little kitten had been jingling on the keychain ever since that Christmas. I touched my fingers to the pendant and gently held it between my thumb and fingers. Hello Kitty's beady black eyes stared up at me, dull and lifeless. I let her drop and repositioned my hands on the steering wheel.

I found myself thinking a lot about my past: retracing all of my steps, all of the choices I had made, and all of the choices others had made, all of them intersecting, reacting with one another like chemicals, and bringing me to where I was: flying down a highway to my therapist, debating whether or not to careen into a tree or a telephone pole.

I nearly missed Sonya's road, and Hello Kitty banged against the dash as I made an abrupt turn.

On the phone Jesse had said we'd had sex six times. It had been five. He had never been good at tracking any sort of information that did not relate to trees, weed, or winter sports. He was amazingly oblivious; I was hyper alert. We had always been an odd pair. One of those odd pairs that *just worked,* as everyone said.

Forest was out in the yard. She pranced about the car while I turned it off and gathered up my thoughts, emotions, and purse.

"Hi, honey," I said softly to Forest as I rumpled her ears. She pushed her snout into my side and purse, smelling Victoria. "Yes, hello," I said.

Sonya opened her office door wide and Forest zipped in ahead of me.

"How is the Seroquel working for you?" Sonya asked once we had seated.

"It's not," I said. "It's not working for me. And I can feel the stability that clonazepam gave me slipping away."

"I'm sorry to hear that," Sonya replied, her face shaping into genuine concern. "Could you make an appointment with your doctor and discuss an alternative option?"

Yes, yes, I *could* do that. It was simpler said than done. Yes, I could call up Dr. Allis, make an appointment, go to the appointment, get a new prescription, fill out the prescription, and try a new medication. I would wait weeks for its effects to be known. But days were hemorrhaging away. Time had become a real entity living in my house. Something I didn't want in my body was growing inside of me. It would be outside of my body in a matter of months, and then I would be fastened to it forever.

I finally sighed. "Yes, I guess that's the most logical next step."

"For being a psychological and emotional wreck—your words, not mine—you are awfully logical about most things."

I thought about this. "I guess I'm a psychological and emotional wreck at all times, except for the few seconds it takes to make actual decisions. I want to make good choices despite the everyday living being a disaster. If that makes sense."

Sonya smiled a little. "I think I understand that."

"I'm too afraid to not make logical choices. Sometimes I think my fear and anxiety simultaneously ruins and saves me."

"But perhaps without the fear you could still save yourself," said Sonya. "Not all decisions need to be made based on fear, yes?"

I nodded but said, "All of mine are."

"Yes, I know many are right now, unfortunately. Can you think of a decision that you've made from a place of freedom? No stress or anxiety factoring into it?"

I pulled a couch pillow over my stomach. "I may be thinking for a long time."

Sonya simply waited.

My mind naturally circled thoughts of Jesse, then tighter, zeroing in on him like a marble swirling around and around a funnel until finally slipping down the hole.

"My decision to date Jesse wasn't based on fear," I finally said.

"Good," said Sonya. "What was the decision based on since it wasn't based on fear or anxiety?"

I shrugged. "I just wanted to. We got on well, I felt safe with him. I thought he was really cute. And ..." I shrugged again. "I just wanted to. I was excited to date him and excited to call him my boyfriend."

"You were excited because nothing in particular scared you about him or gave you anxiety?" Sonya said this as a half-statement, half-question. "The warning siren of anxiety wasn't blaring."

"Yes," I replied. "It felt natural to choose to date him. I guess I didn't overanalyze it."

"That makes sense. What do you think causes the warning siren to go off again and again?"

"An oversensitive spirit," I said. "And a chemical problem with my brain."

"Those are some of the factors, yes. And when is the anxiety siren unnecessary?"

"When there is no real danger."

"I know it's easier said than done, but it would be good to consciously note the things that your logical brain knows not to be dangerous. Once you identify some instances when the alarm is misfiring, this is when you can implement techniques you've learned to muffle the noise of the alarm." Sonya said. "Cognitive behavioural therapy, meditation, hobbies, medication, exercise, putting the right nutrition in your body, and the list goes on. But what if that anxiety alarm, though muffled now, is still there?" Sonya smoothed back a few loose strands of hair that had escaped the clip at the back of her head. "What then?"

From what I could remember, I had never heard this line of reasoning from a counsellor before and I felt the question grow larger in that room. Sonya had put into words a fear that had taken up residence in the recesses of my mind. "Well I suppose," my voice pushed through the heavy air of the question in front of me. "One would have to learn to live with it."

"I think you are right," Sonya said. "This idea may look like defeat on its surface, and so I will do my best to explain. In my experience, some sufferers of anxiety believe that they need to remove anxiety. But I don't think this goal is helpful for them. Many times when anxiety comes to us, there is a fear of the anxiety itself in addition to what the anxiety is about. The cloud of anxiety looms just in front of us and the reflexive action is to fight the anxiety, beat the cloud of anxiety up, squish it down, make it smaller, reason with it to make it leave. But I would like to say this, Imogen. It may be that one could walk through that cloud. Could you remain on the course you were on and do what you were going to do anyway? Yes, the anxiety is thick, but could you merely give a nod to that powerful fear and do as you please anyway? Perhaps we don't always have to fight the anxiety down before we do what we had intended."

Sonya stopped talking and only a comfortable silence ensued.

"I would encourage you to first focus on turning down the anxiety alarm with the resources you have. But, at least for the time being, do not try and stop the anxiety."

Sonya set her pen down on the table beside her; she had not used it once since I had arrived. "I am aware that this may seem like I am telling a fish to fly or a penguin to run. I know this may seem like an impossible, callous approach, and I do not want to sound as though I am disregarding your fear and discomfort. But this is my challenge: in the next few weeks, choose one event or circumstance that gives you anxiety, and simply see if you can just walk through that cloud. Do you think you could do that?"

In truth, I had felt an inkling of inspiration as Sonya spoke. A part of me would always latch onto any kind of remedy because they were a struck match in a black cave. A ray of hope to reach for. "I think I can do that," I said.

"Alright," Sonya smiled and folded her hands around her knee and leaned back in her chair. "I would encourage you to put anxiety in its place. Make it smaller. Give it a silly name. Anxiety may be taking up several rooms in your life, but you own the house."

I let the hair that had been falling around the side of my tilted head stay in its place, not willing to brush it away and look up.

"Anxiety can be fine in moderation. When do you think anxiety could be useful?" Sonya asked.

"When it gets you to use protection during sex," I replied immediately and then recoiled like a turtle retracting into its shell.

Sonya seemed to know that I hadn't meant to say it; it was merely simmering at the top of my thoughts and had slipped out like steam from a pot. She gracefully nodded but stayed silent.

After several beats of silence, I realized she had no intention of being the next to speak.

I sighed. "But we did use protection. It's not like figuring out what happened will change anything, I know that. But it's just infuriating to not know. You know?" I trailed off, turtle into its shell again.

"That's quite understandable," said Sonya. "If something happens in your life that has such a great impact, it's only natural to want to understand every piece." She picked up her pen again. "This is obviously bothering you, so should we continue to talk more about this?"

"Okay," I said quietly.

"Alright," Sonya folded her hands. "Where would you like to start?"

I held my hand up to my cheek in an attempt to hide just a little. "I don't know when I could have actually gotten pregnant. We used condoms every time. And yes, I know condoms can break, and they aren't one hundred percent effective." It felt odd to speak openly about this and I suddenly became a blushing nun. "But I just never thought that this could happen to a couple if they made sure to be safe."

Sonya kept at her vow of silence.

Words continued to come out of my mouth. "We had sex five times. Although, I don't know, Jesse said six times, I'm not sure why. Anyway, that's beside the point. But that's what he said on the phone."

Sonya wrote something down and kept her lips sealed.

"I wish I could just talk with him, period. It's just like I have no fucking support—sorry, I'm sorry—from him." I rested my elbow on the armrest of the couch and laid the side of my head on my upturned palm. It felt good to express the pent-up frustration and anger that had been smouldering inside me like an inferno ever since Jesse had cut me off from his presence and asked me to not reach out again until I made a decision.

"Why is Jesse offering no support?" Sonya asked.

"Because I'm not even allowed to talk to him right now."

Sonya looked up. "I'm sorry, can you explain that further? Why can't you talk to him?"

"What? Oh." I sighed and felt tired to the bone. I guess I had never explained this to Sonya before. "Jesse doesn't want to have a baby. He will continue dating me if I choose to have an abortion, but we're over if the baby is kept."

The explanation was not long. It was that short and that disastrous all at once.

"And Jesse doesn't want to discuss anything until I make my decision," I added. "So we haven't been in contact with each other for …" I closed my eyes. "Many weeks now."

"I'm sorry," Sonya said. "That's a very difficult situation to be in."

"It's devastating." I bit my lip and felt weak and tired. Saying this out loud was like aggravating a fresh wound that had just stopped bleeding; now the blood flow was springing to life again.

"Have you tried reaching out since? Perhaps it was an emotional overreaction?"

"I guess it could have been. But then wouldn't he have reached out to me?"

"Hmm," Sonya nodded. "That's true."

It was my turn to nod and stay silent.

"I guess I could try and text Jesse," I finally said. "See if he responds."

Forest bonked her head on the side of Sonya's chair as she repositioned in her sleep. Sonya looked down at her dog, but Forest remained in a deep sleep.

"I don't particularly understand why it matters, but it matters," I said.

"What matters?" Sonya inquired.

I had given no context, simply verbalized an inner thought.

"I don't know if it's my OCD or my anxiety that's trying to figure everything out to make things feel safer, but it bothers me a lot to know that we used protection every time we had sex, and yet I don't know when I got pregnant."

It was like living on this goddamn planet without knowing *exactly* how life began. Infuriating.

The sun was shining its last farewell for the day as I stepped out of Sonya's door. Forest's tail happily *bang, banged* against the wall as she and Sonya saw me off.

Goodnight, honey, I thought in my mind and tried to telepathically send the message to Forest. Animals deserved every good thing.

The sun, a halved orange, was so low in the sky that the light hardly touched the earth on which I stood.

The headlights of my car illuminated the road in an eerie manner. I was tired and kept my eyes steady on the road as I flipped through several radio stations. My car seemed to have a knack for picking up country music stations and very little else. Maddening. I gave up and turned the radio off. Silence filled up the air quickly, like water seeping into a sinking car. I felt the familiar dread creeping up my body—first at my shins, then my knees, inching up to my waist.

You need to text Jesse, I thought. Once such a mundane occurrence that was natural and safe, now a minefield. What might I say that would drive him even further away? Choose wisely, tread carefully.

The drip, drip, dripping of the anxiety was collecting around my waist and moving up to my chest and heart. A panic attack was a glass cube enclosure, an unforgiving dimension. You can see everyone and everything just as they had been before, but you are no longer *connected* to anything but fear. I had tried on several occasions to explain to Roslin what pure terror felt like, but words could not encapsulate it.

My mind inevitably tried to find comfort somewhere, anywhere. Like a bird looking to nest, my mind flipped through old memories, looking for a hospitable one to land on. If good things had happened in the past, then surely more good things would come.

I could feel Jesse's skin on my skin, just as it had been before. I remember being shocked and thrilled when we were first intimate, his skin was so soft. My rugged Jesse, so soft. His lips were warm and parted so gently against my own. The muscles under his skin moved when he dragged me toward himself. I could hear my sighs fill the quiet air when he contorted my body in bed to meet his own, when I bit his neck, wrapped my legs around him and held fast.

The sound of tires hitting gravel too fast made me touch down to Earth again, and my hands instinctively gripped the steering wheel hard to right the car back onto the paved road again.

The oddest thing happened as tears streamed in rivulets down my face. My chest heaved, and yet I hardly made a noise. I was like a dead body crying.

The shadows created by the car's headlights rose, morphed, and collapsed upon themselves as I drove on.

I thought about Jesse and I intertwined like a pretzel, watching movies, drinking wine, aghast when we went to the kitchen for a second bottle only to realize we were all out.

"Ah well," I had said and thrown myself at Jesse's chest, pulling him in tight, looking up at him with doe eyes. "You have me."

I remembered waking up in the wee hours of the morning at Jesse's house and hearing his deep breaths, gentle and vulnerable. A little lamb fast asleep.

I remember waking up groggy and dizzy the last night I had spent with Jesse, a mere three calendar flips behind us now.

I had woken up with distinct pain in my body, aching all over. My arms, my chest, my stomach, my lower stomach, my vagina, my legs.

I had gotten up, with much difficulty, to pee. I had sat on the toilet, letting my tired and heavy head fall to the side to rest on the bathroom counter. I was hungover, exhausted, and my whole body felt bruised somehow, like I had been thrown against a cement wall. And I couldn't pee. There was pressure down there as if I had to go.

I felt the river of tears slowly dry up, their salty courses making my skin feel tight.

I killed the engine immediately upon parking in my driveway. The headlights died and a silence washed over everything. I sat there for several minutes, staring straight ahead as the pitch black began to form into the familiar shapes of the backyard and the neighbours' yards and fences.

Still looking forward, I reached my hand toward the door handle and clumsily opened the door in a zombie-like state.

Victoria chirped and hummed around my ankles. Tripping hazard. I bent down to pet her fuzzy body and she happily pushed her face into my hand again and again. I half picked her up, letting her back two paws stay put on the floor. Victoria's steady little heartbeat beneath my thumb grounded me, and I held her until she felt the hug was too long and struggled to get away.

I picked up my laptop that sat on the coffee table and opened a new tab, typing in how I had felt that morning at Jesse's. After several minutes I turned on some classical music. *Claire de Lune* played over and over.

I sat in my dark apartment with a solitary lamp shining down on me as I dawdled around the world wide web. I searched a few key words that related to the aches and pains I had felt the morning after Anna and Kieran's party. Medical sites, personal blogs, and comments written by women filtered onto my screen from the search. I briefly felt relieved, unexplainable body pain happened.

The brief elation froze like ice as I continued reading.

Some women wrote that the pain was the result of sexual assault—they had been drugged or passed out when it happened.

151

One had immediately suspected that some sort of sexual foul play had occurred and had gone to the hospital for a rape kit test.

This was not in the realm of possibility, only what an algorithm thought I was looking for.

I punched my knee to bring myself back down to Earth and then slammed the laptop closed. The regret of searching online settled in the air until I wanted to throw plates against the wall.

I did none of those things. Instead I cooked dinner: some pasta, some steamed vegetables, a peach and some dates for dessert.

And then I crawled under the covers of my own bed. This bed was safe and warm.

I stared at the ceiling for a time, but after a while, I brought out my laptop again, thinking I could find a distraction. The screen was just as it had been left, of course: Ontario Coalition of Rape Crisis Centres. I closed that tab on my web page and browsed through all sorts of mindless entertainment instead.

My body was numb but my mind was on fire.

I thought about the alcohol haze that I swam in that night of the party. Me, a lightweight, drinking out of uncomfortable boredom at first, and then to numb the building anxiety. I vaguely remembered trudging into Jesse's house in the early morning. The sleeping pill. Out like a light. I don't know what it would've taken to wake me up. The rapture, perhaps.

I put the laptop down and fell asleep.

And in my sleep I stood on a wooden floor. Unfinished pine, the rings and veins of the tree that once was now weaving through the floorboards beneath my bare feet. The dream state limited my vision and nothing immediately came into view. I turned, trying to see what was around me. This room was large, square, and empty, save for the table in the middle of the room. I went over to the table, and found a milk-white candle. A gentle smell filled the home, growing stronger the nearer to the candle I was. Mint tea, cotton sheets, bookshelf dust, chocolate brownies, lemon-scented floor cleaner.

The room was smaller now, the walls and floor presenting everything familiar and lost. My childhood bedroom. An ache of comfort and sadness and love bloomed.

Then a faint rustle and a little murmur. I turned around to see myself in my little girl-sized body, head bent in concentration over a stack of school papers. I was playing pretend—a teacher marking papers. Wispy bits of hair came loose from a purple hair elastic.

The blackboard on the wall was filthy with chalk dust, well-used and well-loved. I had a desk with my own marked school work piled high, and I taught from there. I was a kind yet strict teacher. I wrote down all my students' names and placed them on my bedroom floor in pairs.

My dream consciousness was pulled from my body; now I was looking onward at my little girl self and my adult self. There was an axe, it materialized during a blink of my eyes. Or rather it had been there the entire time, painted masterfully well to blend in with the floor, baseboards, and wall. Then the axe head blushed fire-engine red and I saw it.

The child in the room was now turned toward the chalkboard, wiping away the last assignment. The adult Imogen watched for a moment, hazel eyes trailing after the little girl's movements. The quietude ended as metal gently grazed wood—the axe picked up off the floor, gripped in the woman's hands and then raised.

My consciousness threatened to break into the woman's body, instinctively horrified. Yet the horror dissolved, first into empathy and then into grief. The little one should not grow older. The muted freckles across the cheekbones, the dissimilar ears pushed flat against the head, the hair like a silkworm's muddied silk should not age, should not reach adulthood.

The world shifted, rearranged itself, and I was no longer looking into my childhood bedroom but the whitewashed room with its pine floors.

I blinked, back inside my body. I half turned toward the square table in the middle of the room, a lick of saffron flame burning atop the white candle.

And then I was coming to the surface, like a body floating up to the surface of a lake, ethereal light gently sparkling through the top of the water. I was waking up, I felt it, and my time in the dream world was slipping away.

I need to kill her, I thought. I fought with my mind to go back to my childhood room, and it obeyed.

My adult arms still held the red axe high over the child's head.

My younger self, a child on the floor, began to tilt her head upwards. I awoke just before her eyes reached mine.

The night shirt I wore was sweaty, the cotton sheets twisted tightly around my frame, my breaths short and erratic. *I didn't kill her. Fuck!* I screamed in my head. If that dream had been a portal in time, and if I could have killed my younger self in that dream, then I would have failed the mission.

I did not dissolve into dust, I did not die, I remained on Earth.

I sighed and rolled over to check the time on my phone. It was just after four in the morning.

I begrudgingly left the warmth of my bed and quickly put my hair in braids. I slipped on my Nike runners and peaked out the front window to gauge the weather's mood. Like a snake, the earth had shed its spring skin entirely. It was summer, in all its stifling glory.

I drummed my fingers lightly across Victoria's head to tell her good morning and that I would be leaving the house for an hour.

The light world, the human world, was on the other side of my door. I blinked at the brilliance of the sunlight.

One Nike in front of the other, let's go.

Images from the dream remained vivid in my head.

I ended up in the vicinity of Victoria Park, and decided I may as well walk through it. Ducks were everywhere, littered around the edges of every pathway like confetti from a birthday party. They looked at me with calm, beaded eyes, used to the human form traipsing around their territory. I wondered what they thought of us, the tall featherless beings that endlessly walked round and round this large pond.

I didn't think birds or animals were either happy or unhappy when they were pregnant. It was only an event in their limited lifespans. I didn't think birds or animals raped one another either. From what I knew from school and documentaries, they all seemed to be well aware of social cues and knew when they were wanted and unwanted.

My heart began to rot as the newness of the day wore off.

In a lightning-fast decision to head back home, I turned on my heel.

I had to speak with Jesse. Yet how could our relationship ever resume if I were to accuse him or even suggest that he might have done something so wrong while I was sleeping? I was already pregnant with a baby he didn't want. Asking him if he had had sex with me while I was asleep would be the fatal blow.

To say nothing was unthinkable.

My obsessive thinking echoed through every chamber of my mind, each fear amplified by another, multiplying rapidly. Pregnancy had made the labyrinth much larger, the way out much smaller.

Did I have relations with a rapist? Was Jesse not still Jesse? Was my Jesse a predator? Even when certain memories of him still caused me to smile? Even when he would point out the most minute things and would construct an entire idiotic story behind its existence? And I would laugh and beg him to shut up for a minute.

"If you were the Prime Minister—" Jesse had asked once. "—what is the first thing you would do?"

"I would take away your freedom of speech because everything you say is criminal," I had told him. And then I had him laughing. I liked to be the reason for his laughter.

A small part of my heart leapt upwards every time a text appeared on the screen of my phone. It was never Jesse. I watched as his name got pushed down further and further on the list of text messages. From time to time I made the mistake of reading through our old texts.

The image of Jesse was being rearranged in my mind, the forgetting of a song, the wind blowing over a pile of leaves, bits and pieces picked up, fewer returning to their place.

I penned multiple drafts of messages I could send to Jesse. I never typed these messages on my phone to avoid an accidental send. I scribbled the messages on scraps of paper and the backs of receipts, crafting sequences of words to ask my boyfriend of three years if he had raped me. Each day didn't feel like the right day to ask, and I would put it off until the next day.

I spent an evening over the toilet bowl throwing up. It was not morning sickness, it was not the baby. It was the physical manifestation of stress.

And then I couldn't stand it any longer. I went to the kitchen and opened the Drawer of Nothings where I had stashed away all of the drafts I had written.

I read through a couple of my scribblings and decided on one. It was the most delicately worded. Not accusatory, more of a question out of pure curiosity than anything else.

I sat down on my bed with my feet dangling over the edge and wrote a message to Jesse for the first time in weeks.

I pressed send and threw my phone to the opposite side of the bed as if it had burnt my hand.

"I will survive this," I whispered.

Sometimes one merely had to believe that they would survive and go through the motions of living until their mind matched the resolution. You had to be determined to lead yourself to safety, you had to hope your body would follow.

I filed my nails, I added some kibbles to Victoria's food dish, I read a few poems, I wiped away the dust from my bookshelves.

And then I heard the unmistakable vibration of my phone and my heart leapt into my dry mouth. I inched toward the phone that lay where it had fallen when I threw it; picking it up carefully, it had all the fragility of an active bomb.

It was Roslin asking if I wanted an old t-shirt of hers that I had once said I liked. My heart began to return to a normal rate as I texted her back. And then the phone vibrated again as I held it with both hands. Jesse. I opened Jesse's text in an instant and stared at the words, seeing them but not comprehending.

Hey. Yeah I think we had sex that night. I was still a little drunk. But yeah we had sex.

I did not foresee this. I had anticipated denial, anger, or curses but not a simple reply like this. Not an admission.

I stood rooted to my bedroom floor.

I had been very drunk that night as well. I was nodding off as Jesse drove us home, my heavy head hitting the passenger window multiple times, waking up only briefly to right myself again in the seat. I had more or less been sleepwalking between the truck and Jesse's bedroom. Had he not seen that?

I had peeled off every layer of clothing but my underwear and left everything in a crumpled pile before I threw myself onto my usual side of the bed. Out of habit I took a sleeping pill from the nightstand drawer. And then sleep followed within seconds and I did not wake up until morning.

My shaking fingers were not doing my bidding as I tried to type a response.

I fell asleep as soon as I was in bed, I replied. *I was asleep.*

I leaned my back against my bedroom wall. Jesse's ghost materialized as it often did in my mind: in my bed, beside my bed, turning off the bedside lamp. This had all happened.

Many times I had curled up beside him, laid my head on his chest, picked up his arm to wrap it around my body, pushed myself into his side for warmth on a winter night, buried myself in the essence of him.

A dark blood stain was beginning to seep into these memories.

I saw that Jesse was typing before I quickly turned off my phone and sank to the bedroom floor.

Each memory of him was framed and hung neatly. They looked so nice against a crisp white background. Each of them was beautiful.

I felt a funeral in my brain.

157

Blood began to bloom on the ceiling above the pictures, as if a bathtub upstairs had overflowed. The thick crimson became too much for the ceiling to hold and began to trickle down the walls, enveloping the framed pictures. They were being ruined.

Another vibration from my phone. Jesse's text: *You know we didn't have that much time together when I was home last. We hadn't had that much sex tbh. What do you want me to say?*

I put my forehead on my knees. I began to feel very sleepy. And then I felt emotionless, and this is when I felt I was stable enough to text back.

Do you not understand the gravity of this? I needed to choose my words wisely, not scare him away just yet.

Gravity of what? Jesse responded.

The gravity of having sex with someone who is asleep or passed out. Now the conversation was flowing. No pauses.

I didn't think you were fully asleep idk.

A blasé 'I don't know'. Fuck you, 'I don't know'.

Well I was asleep. Or passed out. I replied.

Honestly I can't remember much. You're saying that you would've turned down sex that night? Doubt it.

That line of logic is neither here nor there. Maybe I would've, maybe I wouldn't have.

You're my girlfriend. Yeah, it would be fucked up for me to fuck a girl I don't even know, but I know you, and you don't usually turn me down.

I don't know what to tell you. I felt I was talking with someone I didn't know. *There was no consent. I do not want anyone on this planet having sex with me if I am not awake and fully aware of what is happening.*

Jesse didn't text back immediately this time.

I waited for several moments and then started typing. *Do you understand that everything is based on consent? Someone looks after your babies because you consent to them being your babysitter. A bank holds onto your money because you consent to having an account with them. Consent is the fabric of civil society, and the only reason that the word consent needs to be so tightly connected to sex is because you have been so fucking poorly socialized that you have to be taught this over and over again. You are so unbelievably stupid. We don't have to remind men not to murder the children while we're out of the house, why do we have to remind you to not rape?*

158

And that was it.

Jesse texted back, but I didn't read it. I knew what I needed to know. I had nursed a dwindling flame of hope that we would come back together again, maybe even stronger than before if the pregnancy would have only intertwined our lives all the more. But I quietly licked my thumb and forefinger and snuffed out that flame. Jesse would be dead to me from then on. Emotions would still be attached to him for a long time, despite what my mind told my heart. But soon, those emotions would also wither and die. Sever off the limb to save the body.

I stood up from the comfort of the bedroom floor and stared into space as I began to unbraid my hair. In a state of traumatic numbness, I brushed my teeth, I washed my face. I changed into my largest oversized night shirt. I crawled under the covers on my bed. I gently placed my hand atop the tiny bump of my stomach. My tummy was soft and smooth. I thought about what was underneath my hand: skin, fat, muscle, organs, something else the size of a plum, and a little umbilical cord. I then thought in reverse: the plum grew smaller—now a walnut, now an olive, now a pea, now a sesame seed.

And then my own egg and then unwanted sperm.

My stomach twisted up in nausea as I thought about how I had lived in oblivion for three months. I had spent hours agonizing over Jesse's silence. And it was all for naught.

I retraced my steps over the past three years and was revolted by every memory: I had been dating someone who would sexually assault me.

Three years crumbled and decayed into dust.

XII

The cool grey of the early morning was the next thing I saw. It was one of those sleeps that felt instantaneous; the moment after you fell asleep was the moment you woke up. My hand was still exactly where it had been the night before, resting lightly on top of my stomach.

The shadows in my room grew smaller until they vanished as the sunlight crept through my blinds. I swung my legs over the side of the bed after deliberating whether or not to get out of bed that day. I had to pee, and so that decided the matter for me.

My phone rang, the caller ID said it was my mother. I didn't pick up. I had been dodging my parents' phone calls like bullets. When I occasionally replied to their messages with texts, I began with a short explanation that I had been in the shower, driving on the highway, napping at 7pm.

I could not bear hearing their human voices because the little spirit I had left would dissolve and evaporate in the heat of self-hatred.

The last molecules of clonazepam had washed away and I looked on disapprovingly at the Seroquel. The yellow pills were simply inadequate, and more ice was breaking beneath my feet, leaving me on an increasingly cold, small island.

I made more appointments: an appointment with Sonya here, and an appointment with the pregnancy centre there. And my stomach became larger. Some days it was only my own imagination, but other days it was beyond dispute.

I sat down with my laptop one morning and read articles and blogs written by women who had gotten abortions, and women who now had toddlers scurrying around their ankles. Some of the women had known instantly what they were about and simply did what they wanted. Some women changed their minds after a few weeks. Some women had circumstances change, for better or for worse, and some had personal convictions. Few women seemed to be paralyzed with my level of fear and indecision.

I was angry at myself for my own indecision. And I was angry that my mental health was suffering and deteriorating like a plant without water.

Later that day I suffered another severe panic attack. Walls caved in, my vision grew dim, and I was left on the floor on my hands and knees, gripping onto the tiles of my kitchen for dear life, the only thing tying me to this earth.

I scrambled to get things done around the house in the two-hour window of energy I had each morning. If I had an appointment that day, I would drag myself out to the car and wearily drive to wherever I needed to go. Once I drove to the pregnancy centre when I had meant to drive to Sonya's. This made me late for my appointment with Sonya.

"Sorry, I drove to the pregnancy centre by mistake," I explained to Sonya as I wearily dropped onto the couch.

I fixed breakfast and ate it in silence. Cars passed by the house, their little engines creating a Doppler effect on loop. The curtains and blinds remained closed. I slept after breakfast, waking up once around high noon when the outside sun was desperately trying to get inside. Daylight had retreated when I awoke again.

It had been three days since I had showered, and I felt dirty. And so, despite the late hour, I began to fill the bathtub with warm water. I felt the steam rise and touch my unwashed face. I pulled off the clothing that had been on my skin for too long and sank into the embrace of the water. My pregnant stomach was a little hill undersea. I *splish splashed* the water until swirling whirlpools were on either side of me. I placed my hand on my stomach and a numb calm took hold.

I propped my back up against the slope of the bathtub and stared at the ceiling until the water began to lose its heat and I had to get out to refill the tub once again.

I left the water running and, still in an indescribable trance, wrapped a towel around myself and made my way to the kitchen. A dog barked from somewhere outside. My hands stretched out and opened the kitchen cupboards like they were French doors. After drinking two glasses of tap water my hand trailed to the back of the cupboard. My fingers touched the familiar triangle of broken glass. I drew the piece of glass out, leaving the cupboards open, and went back to the bathroom. The tub was nearly too full, and I quickly turned the water off.

I dropped the towel to the floor, placed the glass shard on the edge of the wet tub, and slipped back into the water.

The heat of the water barely fazed me, and I slid far enough down to put my whole head under the water's surface. I slipped under, holding my breath for ten, twenty seconds, then came up for air.

Reprieve would be the loveliest thing imaginable. To leave Earth for just a little while to look at the planets and stars suspended in the black vault of time. I would only need to worry about asteroids and dying stars searing clear through my middle.

A silky paralysis wrapped around my shoulders, neck, and head, now dotted with water droplets.

I picked up the glass and turned the shard around gently in my hand to the sharpest point and cut a clean slice through my left wrist. Blood welled up instantaneously as if it had been waiting for the opportunity to get out. I barely had time to think before I saw my right hand rise up again and cut another line on my wrist. It was unexpected and it was dangerous, but I was only connected to my body by a thread. My eyes fell to my stomach. The little mountain that was steadily growing. I let my left arm drop into the bathwater and winced at the stinging flood of water that bit at the freshly sliced flesh.

I still had the piece of glass in hand. I fixed my eyes on my pregnant stomach and in one motion sliced across it as well. My scream echoed through the room.

Blood was rising to the surface of the freshest cut, then joining itself with the scarlet bathwater.

I stood up quickly and began to drain the water. I did not want to sit in blood. The sight of the rosy water twirling lazily down the drain made me feel weak.

"*Fuck*," I whispered now. I stepped out of the emptying tub and reached for my towel. Thoughtless choice; now, a bloody towel.

Hair dripping into puddles of water, I stood waiting for the white blood cells to put an end to the red that refused to stop flowing.

It would take a while. With my good and healthy right arm, which had done the harm, I opened the bathroom door and delicately stepped to the coffee table where *Mansfield Park* rested. I quickly picked it up and scurried back to the bathroom, where I sat on the edge of the tub, the book propped up on my knees to read. The mass-produced paperback copy, its cover design a victim of the 80s, was found at a garage sale years ago. The pages had already been worn out then, but now the pages were even more well-loved as I had read it several times and had declared it to Roslin one of my favourites. I was engrossed in the story, as if I had never read it before, until I realized that the fibers of the towel had dried itself, along with the blood, along the line of the cut on my stomach. I inhaled, bringing my stomach in tight, and peeled the towel away. Mercifully, the blood did not begin flowing again, but the towel merely encouraged a minor resurgence of red.

I kept reading, this time careful to keep the towel slightly away from my cuts.

The blood finally gave up on its bleeding and dried, and I went to bed. Emotions were dull—echoes rather than the noise itself. I did not know that I could ever have preferred pure, distilled sadness to the murky echo of a dull misery.

Several days passed in rapid succession, and I found myself once again at the pregnancy centre, a lady ushering me in for another ultrasound. She was showing me the nine-month pregnancy schedule she had pulled up on her computer screen. She had given me a printed copy of this schedule on salmon pink paper before and instructed me to tack it to my refrigerator with magnets. I had placed it in the Drawer of Nothings.

Ultrasounds were out of body experiences. Cold gel on the stomach, little alien in a grainy fan shape on the screen, nurses speaking to you in exclamation points.

The nurse that did my second ultrasound had long eyelashes and bold eyebrows. I couldn't imagine that she had ever felt like wearing makeup. Her black hair, greying at the temples, was swept up into a loose bun. She carried herself like a saintly being.

She saw the thin ribbon of red that ran halfway across my stomach.

Just practicing a Caesarian section, I wanted to quip. *In case of an emergency.*

Her mood altered, I felt her energy shift, and I was sorry to disappoint her. The nurse quietly ran the plastic scanner, shaped like a hammerhead shark, over the gel.

I was happy for the appointment to be over and clenched the little black and white pregnancy polaroid in my hand as I left the hospital.

When I came home to the apartment, my eyes glued to all the disaster areas. With disgust, I began cleaning. I hadn't swept or vacuumed in ages, and I had simply been throwing all the mail on one corner of my kitchen counter. The sinks were gritty, my clothes were in laundry baskets regardless of whether they were dirty or not. I began shoving clothes back into my dresser and throwing flyers and useless pieces of mail into the trash can. I tried scraping off old crusty lasagna that had welded itself to a plate but to no avail. I whirled around and threw the entire piece of ceramic into the garbage.

Three days later my wrist and hand were lying in a puddle of cherry-red blood, and I knew that I was no longer capable of taking care of myself for the time being. I stared upward from where I had crumpled to the ground. I needed my mother. With my healthy arm holding tight to the edge of the bathtub, I pulled myself into a sitting position.

I texted her since I still couldn't bear to hear her voice over the phone and asked if I could come home for a couple of days. She responded in a *yes, of course, you needn't even ask,* sort of way.

I knew what going home meant and what my parents would soon know. An irreversible canyon would split between myself and them. A bridge could be built or we could walk around the chasm, but the canyon would always exist from then on as permanent damage.

But I needed to go somewhere safe and I needed someone to take over the reins, just for a little while, just so I could rest.

Early in the morning, before the sun was even up, I began throwing clothes in a suitcase, watered all the plants in the house, herded Victoria into her carrier, and climbed into the car.

Victoria enjoyed the car ride as much as she always did, which was not at all.

As I neared the farm, the finality of things steeled and solidified. I would go into the house, as fragile as the finest of China, tell them I was pregnant, tell them Jesse was the father, tell them that Jesse was no longer in the picture, and distort the answers to prying questions.

The sexual assault was a piece of information I had isolated just enough to rarely acknowledge; it was a bush full of thorns to wear heavy gloves around. It nearly felt irrelevant for the time being, like a secondary problem to be dealt with at a later date. I

165

had time to be a sexual assault victim for the rest of my life, but I had a countdown timer directly in front of me.

From Sonya and the various therapists before her, I knew how humans dealt with trauma, and the sexual assault simply could not be dealt with at this time.

The cutting, the blood I was losing, that was more urgent.

Victoria was becoming distraught. The car ride was getting too long. I pushed my fingers through the little prison bars of the cat carrier to calm her.

The familiarity of every tree and grove of bushes, every road sign, every field of beans, was vivid and overwhelming. My trees, my fields, my territory. I was driving on a road just parallel to Jesse's house. When I reached the same longitude, I had a strong urge to hold my breath, like I had as a child when walking past graveyards and funeral homes.

I assumed Jesse had told no one. Why would he?

I pulled into the long driveway leading all the way to my parents' little farmhouse and took my time parking the car and taking my few things out of the trunk, just enough for two or three days.

I pulled at my oversized shirt I had specifically chosen to wear that day, puffing it out around my middle even though my stomach was still small. I opened the back door and stepped inside the four walls of my childhood. The door banged closed behind me in its usual manner and I listened silently until I heard the pitter patter of my parents' feet over the carpeted floors, coming my way.

The usual welcome: "Hello, honey!" Two hugs, one from Dad, one from Mom. I hugged them loosely.

Mom asked if I was hungry and I said that I wasn't.

"Doing okay?" Mom asked as she rubbed my back.

No cause for alarm there, as I was sure they were both under the impression that this impromptu visit was just another minor mental health crisis. These crises happened from time to time, and I would stay with them for several days until the clouds passed over. They were a mini rehabilitation centre, a psych ward where my things weren't confiscated and the caretakers offered love and support rather than visiting hours and jam packets for cold toast. I would play board games with Mom to distract myself, I would read on their couch, I would take long naps in my childhood bed.

"I'm doing okay," I said and offered a weak smile. "The driving really tired me out, that's all."

Victoria exited her carrier with an air of great distaste for being subjected to its confining walls.

The usual opening conversations ensued with a remarkable dance around the fact that I was currently neither in school nor working. I appreciated that they didn't ask. We talked about the farm and the bakery in town that was soon to close its doors forever. I kept my slightly hunched over posture and kept pulling the shirt material out and away from my body.

We had lunch—eggs, peppered tomato slices, cinnamon apple crisp—and I made every move in uneasiness for the rest of the afternoon. I put my bag in my bedroom and read on the couch. And then when I couldn't stand it any longer, I told my mom and dad that they needed to come to the living room. Mom was washing off her soil-covered hands after hours of digging around in the flowerbeds, and Dad was tinkering around at a project in the basement.

I climbed back onto my spot on the couch and clutched a couch cushion to my stomach. My field of vision began to blacken ever so slightly around the edges and I told myself this was not the time for another panic attack.

The assembly of two took their seats on the two chairs opposite the couch. They did not own a television, and therefore; there were indeed chairs opposite the couch. I wished that Sonya was there with me, even if she didn't say a single word. I would've liked the reassurance of her presence at that moment. There was a hum of silence, the house listening in, before the words were forced through the air.

"I'm pregnant." I said, clutching the cushion in a vice grip, strangling all the stuffing inside of it.

The silence ensued again, everything the same as it was before. I glanced up at Mom, onyx pupils, bronze eyes, then

167

reverted my own gaze to the carpeted floor. Her eyes were molten fear.

The immediate questions were about Jesse. *Does he know? Where is he? He does not want to be a father? He's not even speaking to you?*

"When are you due?" Mom asked.

I said nothing.

I forgot to take my medication this morning, damn, I suddenly remembered.

"Mo," Mom started slowly. "We know in this day and age you may be encouraged to end the pregnancy. Your doctor has probably already given you this option with information about it."

I thought of the small stack of pamphlets I had pushed into my Drawer of Nothings.

"And we also know that in this progressive society—" Mom let this phrase slip out like a snake. "—abortion is treated like a mundane medical procedure."

She stopped talking and I guessed I was supposed to say something.

"Yeah," I said finally.

"But we know that you know what we believe. An abortion is not just a medical procedure. It's become normalized, of course, so it may feel that way, but what it really is, Imogen, is ending a life."

A small lump of emotion, a smooth blend of despair and rage, began to form at the back of my mouth. *"Yes, I know, I know,"* I wanted to say. *"I know all the arguments, I know why you believe what you believe. I was raised with it, I was taught it. I know."*

Instead I simply shook my head.

"I'm not sure if you have been talking to your doctor about getting an abortion or if you have been considering it, but your father and I strongly advise you to keep the baby." She paused and I remained silent. "I'm sure you already know this."

"Yes," I answered. "I know. I know that defending the sacredness of life means keeping every pregnancy going, full steam ahead." It was not the time for sarcasm, but it was a coping mechanism so easy to fall back on. "So you would be mad at me if I decided to get an abortion?"

"No, we wouldn't be *mad* at you," Dad finally spoke. "But it would certainly be a difficult thing to accept."

I regretted coming. I *knew* this would be their response but to hear it being said was different. Like hearing the first sounds of ice cracking beneath your feet over a deep lake. I could've just gotten an abortion and never breathed a word about it to anyone ever. But that scenario broke down every time at the hands of my guilty conscience.

"I just don't … really get it. You think that all life is sacred, and fetuses are as full of human life as you and me and must be protected as much as you and I are protected. That's the gist of it. Am I wrong?"

Mom and Dad nodded in mild agreement.

"But is that always how it would play out every time?" I put two fingers to my temple and wearily gazed at the floor until it began to swim. "Can you picture something for me? You're in a burning building, and you can either run in one direction and save the person at one end of the building, or you can run in the opposite direction and save the person at the other end of the building. At one end is a three-year-old, and at the other, a fetus. If all life is sacred, then you would have a terrible decision to make. Theoretically, they're both equally human, right? But *instinctively,* that person in the middle of that burning building would run toward the three-year-old kid. I *know* you know that the three-year-old needs to be saved."

I wasn't looking at my mother or father, but I felt their coldness. A tired silence entered the room and secured itself to the air we were breathing.

"So …" Mom began hesitantly and then stopped, as if to consider her words. "Does this mean that you are thinking about ending the pregnancy?"

"I mean—" I shrugged. "I guess I'm considering all my options. I'm not really … in a good way right now." I thought of the scars on my wrists that were hidden under long sleeves. It was June, and I had not considered the weather prior to slashing my skin.

I imagined myself in a hospital bed, hair slick with sweat, post-birthing, the nurses and doctor glancing at the scars on my wrists and stomach, sending up prayers to heaven for the child they had just delivered. *What a terrible mother she is going to be,* they would think. And I would agree with them.

The anger that had been burning in my throat changed into an aching grief. I saw the time and effort of therapy evaporate like mist the moment I couldn't be dedicated to looking after myself.

"What do you mean, you're not in a good position?" Mom asked.

"I mean that I cannot possibly fathom being a mother right now. I have no idea how I could take care of a child. I can barely take care of myself."

"Mo," Dad's voice this time. "All parents feel like that with their first pregnancy. No one knows what they are doing. And besides, there are so many books out there these days to help first-time parents. And we'll help you. Your mom and I will help you."

"No," I said. "You don't get it. This goes beyond just the regular kind of 'I don't know what I'm doing' before a baby is born. This is something else."

In my peripheral vision, I could tell that Dad was looking at Mom.

"I see," Mom began. "I think that line of thinking is common when you're fearful of something. You feel as though you're alone or as if no one has felt the way you're feeling. You know, I had some anxiety before you were born as well. We didn't always feel one hundred percent prepared for your arrival either. But you do it, you face life's fears. And there is always something amazing on the other side of fear. We got you—one of the greatest blessings we could've imagined."

Was it normal to be driven suicidal from pregnancy?

I refused to make eye contact with my parents. My heart would wither and collapse upon itself.

"I don't know," I said. "I don't know what I'm supposed to say right now. I don't want to debate, I just want to go to bed. Truly. I just want to sleep."

"Of course," Mom said. "I'm sorry you're feeling so overwhelmed right now. You get some rest. I made up your bed with fresh sheets last night after you said you were coming home."

My mother was incessantly thoughtful. Almost too thoughtful and kind at times, like a sickly-sweet cake. The feeling of unworthiness could fester.

I gave up my death grip on the couch pillow and trudged upstairs, my parents remaining in the living room where they were seated.

The bed was made up crisp and neat, as only my mother could make a bed. I peeled down the comforter, quilts, the sheet, and cocooned myself beneath their weight. I shut my eyes, but there was not enough darkness. I pulled the covers over my head, the way I had often done as a child in this very bed. Though I didn't want to, I strained my ears to hear any murmurings from below deck. I did not detect a thing from underneath the avalanche of blankets. Eventually exhaustion overtook me, my muscles relaxed, and I fell asleep.

I awoke in a state of confusion. The room was grey with shadow, and I hadn't the slightest clue as to where I was. The fog in my mind slowly dissipated, and I recognized my surroundings: the shape of my jewellery box on the dresser, the cross-stitched rabbit framed in gold on the wall. I was at home in my own bedroom.

The house smelled of pasta and beef and the simmering of onion in olive oil. I had slept the entire afternoon away.

My stomach growled and whined. I stretched my limbs under the covers. In order to eat, I would have to see my parents. I briefly considered waiting them out. I could go back to sleep for a few more hours and go down to the kitchen for food after Mom and Dad had gone to bed for the night. But my stomach felt nearly concave with hunger, and I was a feral animal being lured out of their safety zone by the temptation of food.

I was jarred by a soft knock on the bedroom door.

"Mo?" Mom said softly. "Are you awake? It's supper time."

I stayed still until I finally whispered back, "Yes, I'm awake."

"Are you going to join us for supper?"

"I'll come down."

"Okay," I heard Mom whisper back and then her feet padded down the stairs.

I lamented my fate and dragged limb after limb out of bed.

I tiptoed down the old oak stairs like a burglar in the night and nearly tripped over Victoria as I descended off the last step. She wove her little body between my legs. I scooped her up and decided that she would be my shield, a barrier between my parents and I.

Dad was already seated and Mom looked up at me and smiled as I stepped into the room.

"Did you have a good sleep?" Mom asked.

"It was decent," I said. "I didn't know I would sleep this long."

"You must've been very tired," said Dad.

I nodded in agreement.

Mom was scooping beef stroganoff out into a large bowl, the one I had chipped on the corner of the counter when I was eleven.

Victoria was no longer enjoying being a shield and squirmed to be free of my arms. I wished that I could make her understand that I needed her to stay. I looked at her pale kiwi eyes. *You would never make it as a service animal,* I thought. I gave her one last pleading look and then reluctantly released her. She immediately scurried off into the black void of the dining room. I sat down heavily at the table of food.

The three of us all knew the silent cue to prayer and bowed our heads. Dad blessed the meal and Mom started immediately dishing up steaming roasted vegetables after *amen.*

I wanted to follow Victoria's lead, grab a plateful of food for my empty stomach, and skitter off to my room again. Instead, I used the salad tongs to scoop up heaps of lettuce. My mind dulled and wandered around to a memory I associated with the aroma of the kitchen. I found myself with a full plate of salad. I smiled slightly as though I had meant to do just that.

The dinner proceeded, and I soon realized that we would not be talking about the news I had delivered to them. Mom and Dad kept the topics of discussion stabilized around the farm, the tractor that was beginning to refuse to be a good tractor, the coming fall, the trip to Prince Edward Island that Mom had been wanting to go on for years now, the contemplation of the cost of such a trip, the foreseen close to the conversation (perhaps next year). Mom and Dad lived life with the stoicism of the marbled saints who lived in the corners of gothic churches. With a somber gaze, they looked to the future. I was born and immediately adopted the attitude. It had left a dark stain on who I grew up to be, but I did not know how to get the stain out.

My parents must have privately come to an understanding that they would not speak of the pregnancy until I initiated a conversation on the subject matter myself. This was kind and considerate and maddening. The long-suffering patience of my parents veiled the disappointment, anger, and hurt that I knew they were feeling, but it peeked through nonetheless: in the way Dad drummed his thumb on his thigh, in Mom forgetting to ask me if I would like evening tea, in everything.

Before going to bed for the night I told them that I may be driving back to the city the next day. And by *may* I meant that I would. I couldn't take any more of it.

The next morning, I ate a late breakfast of peanut butter and honey on toast, long after my early bird parents had eaten.

I scooped up Victoria and put her in the cat carrier before she had time to protest. After a quick goodbye, I closed my car door and made a mad dash back to the country roads I had just driven.

It was a windy day. Tree limbs bent and leaves fluttered. Birds looked frustrated with their compromised mobility, cattle congregated together in their muddy fields. I could feel the wind swaying my car. Nature was fluid and expressive, and I liked feeling small in the face of its moods. I had always adored thunderstorms. Lightning and thunder were nature's magic for me as a child, and I would peer out our windows during rainstorms and silently wait and hope for more magic.

Weighty panic was pressing down on my chest, constricting my airways. My brain felt like it was filling with water. And I was trapped in that brain like a person trapped in a car sinking to the bottom of a lake, the water pressure already pushing against the car, the doors impossible to open.

With each passing kilometre, I felt it worsening, and I began to dread the idea of facing an empty apartment and being the only human overseeing Imogen.

A car passed me because I had slowed too much, putting more time between myself and the apartment.

I slammed my hand against the steering wheel. *I can't. I can't go.*

Another car passed me as I pulled to the side of the road. There was a little dirt laneway for a farmer's tractor that led to a field, and I steered the car there. Victoria instantly began uselessly pushing at the carrier's door.

"No, no," I placed my hand on top of the carrier. "We're not home."

We were halfway between my parents' country house and my apartment. I could go on or I could go back. I laid my head back on the headrest. I wasn't sure if I would try to hurt myself when I got to the apartment.

I pulled both my feet up onto the seat and tried to hug my knees to my chest. I had to set my feet a little wider apart on the seat, making room for the curve of my stomach. I prayed that no driver would see me and be alarmed. My next vehicle needed tinted windows.

"Okay," I finally said out loud. "I have to go back." I put the car in reverse, pulled out of the little laneway and headed west, retracing my path. As uncomfortable as it was to be under the same roof as my parents, being without them would be even worse.

Alarm and confusion lined the two faces that peered at me once I was on the other side of the door. Mom immediately asked what was wrong and did I need some orange juice. I declined.

"I had a panic attack and I can't be alone right now," I whispered into her hug.

That evening I drove to the lakeshore. I took my shoes off and waded a little ways into the water.

I curled my toes into the sand and stood with my face against the wind. After some time, I closed my eyes and tried to access a different consciousness—just for a little while, I wanted to see if I could do it. This consciousness was contained in a single sparkle of light and it could go anywhere it wanted. It was as light as air itself and could float along lazily, like a leaf in a stream, or it could jet off to the tropics, to Antarctica, to anywhere. It wasn't tied to a body.

Another day died. I collected myself piece by piece until I was able to pad back to my car, my feet still bare and now caked in cool sand.

We had still not spoken any further about my pregnancy, neither my parents nor I had uttered a word about it that day. But this facade did not have longevity.

It wasn't until later, when I was laying on my back, staring up into the blackness of my bedroom that I remembered: appointments. Appointments coming like arrows. I was supposed to see Sonya on Friday, and the lady at the pregnancy centre had somehow conned me into setting up another appointment with her as well. She had mentioned some medical terms, a birth plan, and other prenatal shit that I hadn't understood.

The next morning was scrambled eggs, orange slices, and a precarious armistice. The three of us ate in our own quiet worlds, each of us only speaking several sentences the entire meal. I held a mangled mess of frustration in my chest.

Oh, are we mourning the death of the baby already? I wanted to scream.

I rinsed off my plate and placed it in the dishwasher. *You may be mourning the death of your daughter soon, the way things are going,* I thought.

I felt as if I had walked in on a heated argument—both sides screaming at the other, both believing their opponent was committing mortal sin. And then there was me: in the middle of things and not knowing, thus disappointing both sides, a friend to neither.

It was near the end of that afternoon that the dam broke; I said my stomach was feeling a little off and Mom asked if it was because of the baby. Pandora's box was unlocked.

"No, it's not that," I said. "I think it's because I didn't take my supplements with food." It very well could have been the baby, but I did not want to say this.

"Oh, I see," Mom nodded. "Have you had much morning sickness?"

I shrugged. "Some, I guess. It hasn't been too bad."

"You've been seeing your doctor regularly for the baby?"

"Yes. And I've been having regular appointments at a pregnancy centre."

Mom's eyes flickered. Pregnancy centres were synonymous with abortion clinics to her—a middle man industry that advised pregnant woman after pregnant woman to end their pregnancies, to be selfish.

Mom adjusted herself and rearranged her facial expression into a placid smile. "The pregnancy has been a healthy one so far?"

Did she mean for the baby or for me? "Yeah," I said. "It's been healthy so far."

"That's good," Mom said. "I'm glad to hear it. Is there … anything I can do for you and the baby?"

We were a dynamic duo now. And I had lost autonomy.

"No," I said and regulated the sarcasm in my voice. "I think we're good."

I tried to busy myself around the house, making it look as if I had adult-like responsibilities to take care of including painting my toenails and making a curry. My mother began to assume greater parental responsibilities over me than had been in place when I was a teenager. I should be doing this and not that, eating more of this and less of that. She was kind in every word she spoke, everything rooted in care and concern.

I made a hushed phone call to the pregnancy centre behind my closed bedroom door to change the date of my upcoming appointment. I let Sonya know that I was at my parents' home, that I wasn't entirely sure when I would be coming back to the city, but that I would set up another appointment with her as soon as I could.

"I have some of your old baby things stored away in the attic, you know," Mom said one afternoon. "I'd be happy to bring them down, and you can see what you need."

I had harboured a small hope in the back of my mind that I would end the pregnancy; somehow, I would make peace with myself, the war in my mind would tire and end peacefully on its own. I would be free to choose. This had not happened. The sun kept setting on all my days. Time did not pause, the turmoil continued.

I tilted my head in the slightest nod. "That would be alright."

"Good, good," Mom said happily and her eyes sparkled. "I'll do that this evening."

I smiled weakly.

I needed my parents even though it hurt to be around them. They sustained me and yet injured me. Poison mixed with medicine.

I *knew* my parents; I knew they loved me still. Always. But I could disappoint them. I could hurt them and they could hurt me. I was terrified of hurting them.

I tied my hair back and went for a walk, down one of the dirt roads that ran parallel to the farm. Tall trees lined the road. It was so hopeful there. Wild wood lilies bloomed in clusters, blooming even in the muddy ditches. Goldenrod grew thickly at the edge of the road. White yarrow mixed in amongst the tall grass. Soon there would be small worm-bitten apples and pears hidden in the tree branches.

I bent down to pick a stem of chickweed from the side of the road. A tiny white flower bloomed at the end of it, small and fragile. It was a wonder that life was sustained, let alone beautiful life. How did they do it? Growing up through sidewalks, bending under violent winds, drowning in downpours of rain. I rolled the little stem gently between my thumb and forefinger as I walked on.

While I was living under the roof of one rhetoric, another goddamn rhetoric pushed its way into my mind, elbows out—autonomy and freedom and choice.

But I had felt guilty since I was a child, and the feeling never left. I nearly wanted to keep the baby to please others. I could never disregard my parents. They had kept me alive. They had done everything for me—found mental health professionals, researched depression, bought medication, accommodated and sacrificed, drove hours to therapists, affirmed my existence when I didn't want to be alive.

I had no desire to be careless with my parents and walk over their opinions like dirt.

I had worn down the stem of the chickweed, and it was now utterly limp in my hand. I gently tossed it by the wayside. The wind had picked up and the sky overhead was debating with itself over whether or not to rain. I had walked far enough and turned back.

XIII

The prenatal appointments and counselling sessions could not simply come to an abrupt halt now that I was not in the city. Because I was fragile like a seeded dandelion and needed to be under supervision, I could not foresee an end to my stay with my parents. The appointments were reinstated, and so I traversed the stretch of kilometers between country and city nearly once a week.

Sonya's beautiful mess of an office was a divine sight—there was the couch, the diverse strains of magazines, the tissue box on the coffee table, and there, under the side table as always, was Forest.

"A lot has happened," I began. Sonya nodded and poised her pen above the note paper on her knees. "I'm staying with my parents for the time being."

Sonya's face didn't change as she wrote, though she was aware of all the anxieties that surrounded that loaded statement. Always the professional. "Things weren't going well. I … wasn't feeling well and didn't want to be alone."

"How weren't you feeling well?" Sonya asked. "What were those feelings?"

"It's a lot to put into words." It was a kaleidoscope of feelings intersecting and echoing infinitely. "I can hardly take care of myself, and some days, I feel so low that even something like folding and putting away laundry feels like a monumental task. Every time I think of a baby being in the same house as me, I feel so anxious I get sick. There is no part of me that feels I can be a mother, let alone a good one. I'm on different medication because of the pregnancy, and the new pills aren't working like the clonazepam had. They just aren't, and everything is getting harder. My parents were out for the evening the other day, and when I opened the fridge to make myself supper, I realized I was too tired to even put something in the microwave. I ended up just going to bed hungry. I feel horrible around my parents, but I need the supervision. My parents don't want me to get an abortion because they don't want to think of their daughter as a murderer. Maybe if I was still on clonazepam, I could handle them—Mom and Dad. But I can feel anxiety seeping into everything, nothing is sealed from it."

"Jesse's out of the picture, so I don't even have someone to share the guilt with. Like he left the crime scene early, so now he's pardoned of responsibility somehow. I don't even think about him much right now because that's how consumed I am with anxiety about the baby. But when I do think about him, I think that I've never been more violently furious at another human being. He's hardly even human to me now. I have panic attacks more often than I ever have. They aren't triggered by specific things anymore, they just come. As soon as I wake up in the morning, intense anxiety sets in. Immediately."

"I used to obsessively check my stomach at the beginning of the pregnancy, to see if a bump was showing, but now I avoid mirrors altogether. When I get out of the shower, I have to turn my back to the bathroom mirror because looking at myself is repulsive. I can't believe it's me, I can't believe my stomach looks like that." An alien flourished from a body I lived in. I wasn't alone anymore; something else grew and gained recognition. A greedy plant, nutrient thief, sun stealer.

Sonya looked off into the distance, her mind in a philosophical trance. "Yes," she said. "Yes, I can understand those things. But I think you are handling this better than you might imagine you are."

I turned the corners of my mouth down and said nothing.

"Here's how I see it, Imogen," Sonya spread her delicate hands across her notebook. "You went home to be with your parents because you knew you needed that support. You go to your doctor for medication because you have decided that is what's best for you. You are sitting here because you consistently seek support and counselling. Would you not be more fragile without these things in your life?"

I indicated that I would be.

"You are showing strength by simply asking for support and finding different tools to help yourself."

"It doesn't feel like strength."

"No, it may not feel like strength," Sonya folded her hands. "But feelings are fickle. We cannot rely on them to dictate the course of our lives. You are strong, Imogen. God, you're strong. You've told me your story, you've told me what you've been through, and I imagine there are some things you haven't shared with me as well. You have stayed afloat despite all these things. You need not question your strength, I really believe that."

I left Sonya's with a bittersweet, acidic taste in my mouth. I half-believed her that I was strong, and I half-believed that I had fooled her into believing I was strong.

I sent a vague SOS message to Roslin. Through a plethora of words that meant nothing, yet encased the sentiment of something, I told Roslin I was sorry I had been distant lately, it was just something I was going through—relationship problems with Jesse mostly.

Roslin herself was busy reading copious amounts of textbooks on civil rights law, bogged down in the depths of a postgraduate education. She responded to texts once a day, usually in the evening, her discipline unfathomable to me.

It was painful to talk to my soul mate who was still unaware of the pregnancy. From time to time, I nearly slipped and broke the news to her, but insecurities ran deep, and I was terrified of the response, worried that her initial reaction would scare me into distancing myself from her. Therefore, I kept her at an arm's length.

Back at home, I baked apple crisp and half-listened to my mother's chatter about the different varieties of birds she had identified at the birdfeeder so far that year.

A text from Roslin reached me on Saturday evening and left me cold.

Someone told my sister that Jesse's coming back home. Did you know this? Roslin still lived in a narrative that had stopped being true several months ago.

My neck and shoulders froze into immovable slabs of stone. *No. When?*

Soon, was her reply. *I'm not sure when. I will text my sister. One sec. Okay.*

I put three servings of apple crisp in a bowl and darted to my bedroom. The cinnamon-sugar goo coated my mouth.

Hours later, another text from Roslin: *Natalie said his plane is landing sometime tomorrow. Don't know when. He said he's coming home for the summer.*

The motherfucker was coming home for the summer.

I bit my lip. Some of my things were still at his place. My grandmother's wedding band was there, the one I had forgotten.

The ring must be retrieved before Jesse returned. Jesse, a careless homeowner, never locked the sliding glass doors that stood between the kitchen and the decaying wooden porch.

I would simply go to his place, trespass quietly into his house, grab my things, and be done.

The hour was just shy of one in the morning, my eyelids heavy.

There was a stone wall encircling all my memories of Jesse, hard cement and water-washed stones. I had built it myself. I told myself that I could disassemble this wall when the time was right because two devastations could not coexist. When thoughts of him threatened to surface, I simply pushed them *down, down* until they gave up and drowned. There was no energy to spare on him, no emotional or mental bandwidth. Yet now I found a fracture in the stone wall—the news of his return—a small break, and water poured through the breach, stirring the memories from their hidden home.

Now loose and rampant wolves, the thoughts made me unsafe in my own head.

I thought about the early days before we had declared ourselves an official couple, when we were merely heading in that direction.

Our relationship had begun gently with an air of reservation. I had never dated anyone before, and while Jesse had, he did not rush or push, merely walked amiably beside me as I figured out what dating was going to be like.

A few days after the first day of autumn, Jesse and I had been standing together on his mother's back porch. No one was home, only Jesse and I and a quartered moon. The chill of a September dusk was setting in shyly, testing out the waters of the new season.

I turned toward the house so that my face would not be against the cool breeze. Jesse was talking about his leg that had been hurting since his hockey game the week before. Then he turned slightly and noticed I was visibly cold.

"Oh," he said, with subdued realization. He stepped toward me and opened his arms. A zip of euphoria ran through my blood as I walked into his embrace. We didn't say anything, and after a few moments, Jesse moved his hand up from my waist to hold my head against his chest. I had forgotten the cold and everything else in the world.

Jesse's whisper, "Do you want to go inside?" broke through my happy reverie.

I had sat down on the living room couch, Jesse beside me, and in unspoken unison we laid down, his right arm scooped me to his side as I rested my cheek on his chest.

A window in the kitchen was cracked open, letting the chilled evening air move silently throughout the house. A few birds sang outside, little violent stabs of noise into a silent evening, an ethereal atmosphere for two humans.

We were boyfriend and girlfriend after that day. We were boyfriend and girlfriend for three years after.

I did not fall asleep until three in the morning and woke up feeling like I may as well have not slept at all. The slant of light did not bode well. Nine o'clock? Ten o'clock? I reached over and grabbed my phone off the nightstand. Nine forty-eight.

I whipped off my pajamas and pulled on the clothes closest to me—the clothes I had worn the day before. I ran a brush through my hair four times before pulling it into a ponytail. I grabbed my purse and ensured my car keys were inside before quickly descending the stairs.

"Good morning," Mom said as she spread blood-red raspberry jam over toast.

"Oh," I said flustered. "Good morning."

"Did you have a good sleep?"

"Yeah," I said without thinking.

"Heading somewhere?"

"I'm just driving to the lake," I said as I tied up my shoelaces.

"Oh, a morning drive to the lake!"

I usually only went in the evenings.

"That's a nice change," she said.

"Yes," I nodded mildly. "It is." I waved goodbye and shut the door behind me.

It was a twenty-minute drive to Jesse's house, and I needed a governor to keep me within reasonable speeding limits.

"I will be there before ten-thirty." I whispered under my breath. "It will take all of five minutes." And then I started fervently praying that Jesse had not been on an early morning flight.

I thought about the last time I drove to Jesse's. If I could have seen into the future, I would not have believed that the next time I would be driving his way would be as a victim of sexual assault. His victim, nonetheless.

A sexual assault victim was now what I was labelled as, and the violently funny thing was that I had done nothing between the moments before becoming a sexual assault victim and the moments afterward. The label did not refer to my actions, only Jesse's. Labels could befall you because of what others chose to do—no intent, no thought, no action necessary on your part. You could be asleep and become part of the sins of others.

A cold revulsion seized at me as I neared Jesse's property, followed by a slow burning of hope as I slowed the car to turn. It was desolate, and only dry, empty air blew around the house.

I turned off the ignition. I was filled with equal measures of fury and sadness. It was a cold fury without red hot anger because there was grief attached. Cold fury mixed with heartache on the painter's palette made a blackened, dirty, midnight blue. Killed every other colour on the canvas.

I opened the car door. The driveway was empty, meaning Jesse had driven someplace to leave his truck and catch a ride to the airport. I could imagine Byron offering Jesse a ride to the airport—*free of charge, son!*—if he left his truck and keys in Byron's possession.

The foundation of the house was continuing to crumble. Snow and rain were eroding the cement, leaving sharp bits and pieces on every side of the house. I felt sorry for the house, I always had. The once proud yellow brick Victorian country home was now a tired homestead, left vacant for months on end. I thought that former owners might cry to see it as it was and hope that someday someone would make it beautiful again.

I walked around to the back of the house where patches of grass lay dead from months of heavy snow. An old barbeque that somehow still managed to grill steak and kebabs sat on the back wooden porch accompanied by several rusting lawn chairs that Jesse's father had so thoughtfully dropped off one summer, leaving without asking whether they were wanted or not.

I reached for the handle of the sliding glass door and pulled sideways. It slid wide open. The air in the kitchen was stale, gone bad like milk. I didn't bother taking off my shoes but strode through the house until my eyes caught on a framed photo of Jesse and I that hung above the couch.

"Of *course*," I said aloud into the dead air. Jesse had not been home since our relationship had died. This house still thought we were together. It still *looked* like we were together. My things were in the closet, my blue toothbrush was beside Jesse's red one, the silver cans of sparkling water that I liked must still have been sitting in the cool basement too.

I turned on my heel and ascended the stairs that creaked in all the usual places. I wanted to go through each room and systematically dismantle every suggestion of a relationship, but there was no time for that.

Get the ring and go, just get it and go.

The ring was not in the jeans pocket I thought it would be in. Nor was it in the pocket of my sweater that hung just beside the jeans. My past moronic self had assumed that it would just be there in the pocket of one of my articles of clothing, that is where my mind had placed it. But it was not there.

I threw the clothes down in frustration and surveyed the bedroom of mismatched furniture. I checked the dresser, then the nightstand next. I branched out into the hallway, the bathroom, the spare room. Frustration and panic set in, and I began to slam doors and cupboards in vexation. I descended the stairs and looked through each room on the ground level, but nothing came of that either. I went back upstairs and started over. This time I picked through everything and wondered if Jesse would notice the rumpled clothes or items facing east instead of north. It was unlikely. He did not notice things.

My fingertips touched cool metal. I pulled the ring out from the bottom drawer of the nightstand and clutched it to my chest. The ring had been pushed to the very back of the drawer, under bits and pieces of Jesse's teenage years.

I slipped the ring onto my finger and quickly rearranged the things in Jesse's bedroom that I had left in the worst state of disarray, acutely aware that I could not look directly at the bed.

I held my hand against my chest, ringed finger over my heart, and fluttered down the stairs like a moth. I opened the sliding glass door and closed it deftly behind me.

Never again, I told myself. *I will never come back here.*

That chapter of my life had closed—hastily, without forewarning, and with the pain of severing a limb, it had closed.

I stepped off the last step of the back porch and heard the familiar growl of the pickup before I saw it flying across the highway. I thought about running to my car and locking all the doors.

He slowed and turned into the long driveway.

And so I stood where I was and did not make any movement toward my car. Fear dropped off my shoulders and fell to the ground like a snake and slithered away. I couldn't be afraid of something less than human to me. Fear of physical harm maybe, but I couldn't be scared of *him*.

The tinted windshield of the truck slowly revealed the outline of shoulders and neck and face until it materialized into Jesse.

I stood there, rooted to the ground, as if I had always been there, as if I owned the property myself.

Jesse shut the truck door behind him. "What are you doing here?"

I looked at him. The true colour of Jesse's eyes had always been indiscernible to me despite how many times I had been consumed by them. They were so dark brown, water at the bottom of a well, that I had always identified them as black. Those black eyes had always made his emotions an enigma. His face stayed neutral, his eyes revealed nothing, and so I mirrored the look, dead-eyed and only just breathing.

"I got my grandmother's wedding ring," I said. "I remembered I had left it here."

"So you decided to let yourself in?"

"Hm," I murmured.

He moved a few feet in my direction. "Found the ring?"

"Yeah."

"Does my house look ransacked?"

"You'll have to see for yourself I suppose."

I watched him step back to lean against the front hood of his truck. A silence ensued and I was happy to say nothing to him.

Jesse's eyes fell to my stomach. "I see you're keeping the baby."

"I haven't decided yet," I said.

"Better not wait too long."

"Better not give advice on a pregnancy you're too scared to acknowledge responsibility for."

"Do you want me to acknowledge responsibility?"

"That would be great actually."

"Okay, fine. I got you pregnant."

I kept my eyes lifeless and unfeeling, divided my emotions from reality and spoke as if I were a third-party observer. "Do you realize what you just said?"

"I'm the father of the baby?"

"Obviously you're the father of the baby. I have never slept with anyone else in my life." I went silent, Jesse stayed silent. The dumb fuck.

"Unconscious people don't make decisions. Do you know what another word for non-consensual sex is?"

Jesse turned his head to the side and swore fiercely. "Do *not* come at me with that bullshit. I did not rape you, you know that. I was your boyfriend." Venom mixed with his breath.

"You've mixed too much alcohol and weed together, haven't you?"

"Alright, stop," said Jesse, his shadow casting long behind him. "You are upset like this because you got pregnant. You're upset about the pregnancy, you're not really upset about the sex."

"I'm upset about both actually."

"For the love of God, get an abortion, it's not hard. This is what you do all the time: you overthink everything, get anxious about everything imaginable, and then me and your friends and your family—whoever—have to be so cautious around you because your whole world is balanced on the edge of a knife. *Oh, what's Imogen going to be scared about this time? Oh shit, Imogen is going to have another panic attack. How can we make life more comfortable for Imogen? How can we structure our lives around Imogen?* It's exhausting. You need serious help." There was a moment of silence. "And don't even think about adding anyone new to your life because you will just kill them too, day by day. It's a slow death with you."

His words pierced me like shrapnel, and I knew I would have to process it all later, see if there was any truth in his hateful words or if they were all fostered in his emotional poverty.

My gaze never left his face, and I waited a few seconds to see if he had any more words to say, but he did not. The morning had turned to afternoon and I needed to go home.

"Okay, rapist," I said mildly.

Though Jesse was looking past me at the wheat field behind his land, I saw spitfire anger fill his body. His jaw tightened, but still, he said nothing.

I moved back as his hand reached out to grab my shoulder and he grasped at thin air. He looked surprised for a split second before raising a fist. I ducked, turned on my heel, sidestepped Jesse, and set off running toward my car. The lump in my throat was gone and pure oxygen filled my lungs. Anger cleared my head.

Light and shadow flitted across the ground. Something was moving, and I thought it was merely the trees in the wind. A taller shadow, one too dark and close for tree branches, emerged before me, rushing eastward to meet my own shadow, nearly eclipsing it.

I whirled around and saw Jesse behind me. His right hand stretched toward me. He had so often reached for me before. At family gatherings, while we mulled around the edges of the room, counting down the hours until an appropriate departure time, he would pull me to his side. In bed during the godforsaken hours of the early morning, he would reflexively pull me toward himself in a hazy half-sleep. His hands had reached for me many times before, in a protective, absentminded manner. I looked at his hand then as it reached for me, wicked hand.

I grasped the car's door handle and pulled. "Jesse—"

His hand curled around my wrist, then yanked hard. Pulling me away from my car.

I threw my keys and purse into the passenger seat through the small crack of the open car door, then turned, clenched my right fist, and met Jesse's face with it.

Early summer sunburnt skin gave way to bone. A stream of blood trickled then flowed down Jesse's chin, his neck, and onto his shirt.

I withdrew my right hand as his own fell away from me.

Jesse held one hand over his nose and mouth, while the other remained dead and motionless at his side.

I watched the blood flow. "If you ever come near me again, I will light your house on fire while you are asleep in it."

I glanced down at my grandmother's wedding ring, pressed tightly against the steering wheel as my hands whitened in a vice grip.

There were many days I doubted were survivable. Violent emotional pain had manifested itself as a stabbing sensation deep in my chest, the knife not slicing into me but cutting out of me. A deadly combustion somewhere between the sternum and spine. My heart was damaged and bleeding internally.

Will I survive this? I screamed in my head. The curtain had been peeled back on my relationship with Jesse to reveal a tragedy.

I drove the long way home to the farm. Birds flitted in front of the car, wildly chasing each other with reckless abandon.

I want to be a bird.

After another fifteen minutes I was pulling back into my parents' laneway. I parked and rested my forehead against the steering wheel, the rest of my body lifeless as a doll. I gathered up the few pieces of retrieved clothing I had found in Jesse's closet, then set them back down again because I couldn't leave with only my purse and come back with an armful of clothes. They would need to stay in the car.

Mom remarked that I must have really enjoyed my time at the lakeside since I had been gone so long. I had entirely forgotten what I had told her earlier that morning.

"Yes," I smiled coldly. "It was beautiful." Time had frozen; the day felt unreal. It was odd to enter my bedroom and find the unmade bed blankets just as they had been when I left.

Over the months, the sound of Jesse's voice had become faint in my mind, but now his voice was at the forefront of every thought. I heard him speak the words he'd said that morning over and over again in my head. I heard the animal speak, yes, but I could not identify the emotions that followed. Heavy, dark, and hollow. But no name for the emotion. I wanted to pick out each piece of shrapnel that Jesse had shot at me that morning and throw them away, but instead I turned the words over and over in my mind, obsessively, relentlessly, until they were as smooth as glass.

I sat upright in my bed ruminating for hours. By evening a new, earthy scent filled the house.

I descended the stairs, drawn by the smell. Several large cardboard boxes sat in the living room, two of them labelled *Imogen's baby clothes, 0 to 6 months,* and the other *7 to 12 months.* A huge box sitting beside the other two read *Miscellaneous toys and keepsakes.*

My stomach soured, yet a sweetness coated my mind. I remembered some of the things that were in those boxes. My favourite pair of pants that I had worn until the seat of the bottoms were threadbare and my pastel underwear peeked through. Tiny scrunchies that had pulled back my wispy toddler hair as I played. A Winnie the Pooh cookbook for children, every recipe needing honey, the tea set from my grandparents, my dad's old t-shirts that I had worn like nightgowns. So much time had passed since my younger self had used these things.

I bit my lip and moved past the boxes and into the kitchen. The most familiar smell saturated the air. I could have identified that smell anywhere: Mom's chicken and rice dish. It smelled like home, it smelled like comfort, it smelled safe.

I seated myself at my usual spot. Dad still wasn't in from working outside.

Mom dished steaming root vegetables into a large serving bowl. "Did you see the boxes?" she asked.

"Oh yes, I saw."

"We can look through them whenever you want to. When I pulled them out of storage, well ..." Mom seated herself across from me. "… my goodness, did they bring back a lot of memories."

I nodded and looked out the south-facing window. I felt tears welling up and threatening to spill onto my cheeks. I blinked rapidly and kept the tears at bay. Outside the window, edges of the southern sky were hinting at what must have been a brilliant sunset in the west.

I thought about myself as a little girl, whose dream it was to be a librarian and read every book under the sun. "There are a lot of books in the world," Mom had told me. "I know," I replied. "But I think I can read them all."

But I would lose all desire to read at age fifteen. One day I finished a book and simply did not start another for three years. From ages sixteen to eighteen, I could hardly distinguish between days. Grey-shadowed bedroom, lost RSVPs for friends' birthdays, distraught mother, prescription drug receipts. Many days were spent in bed. I didn't have hobbies, I rarely saw friends, I had been left behind in the wake of normalcy.

After my seventeenth birthday, I stood in front of the bathroom mirror and swore to myself that I would never bring a child into this world—not ever. A blood oath with myself. I had never wavered from those words spoken to my seventeen-year-old reflection. I was not aware of what the future would hold.

We looked through the boxes, my mother and I. It brought back happy memories; it brought more dread of the future. I ran my fingers through the coarse hair of a baby doll that a relative—we couldn't remember which one—had given me for Christmas. I imagined a new pair of tiny hands dressing the baby doll, brushing its hair, taking it outside to play. Would those hands know to be as gentle with the doll as I had been? Who would my child be? Was it up to me to shape their personality and moral compass? Would they hurt me like I was hurting my parents? Would they grow to hate me and my deficiencies?

Mom helped me sort through everything, holding up items one by one, asking if they would be useful, organizing them into piles on the floor beside us.

I watched as her eyes brightened, her face became animated, and the spark of old memories rekindled in her mind. Life was overlapping on itself, tectonic plates creating a fault line, a break in reality. My mom looked behind at her motherhood, I looked ahead to mine.

As weeks slipped into months, I went back and forth between my own apartment and my parents' home. I began staying in the city for a week and then heading back to my parents for a week. My parents offered to pay half of my monthly rent as my own funds dwindled. They never asked me if I should be getting a job or how I would support myself in the future.

I visited the lakeside like I was visiting a dying relative, only I was in the hospital and the lake was the visiting comforter. I was mesmerized by the water's strength, fragility, and persistence. The waves never stopped, they went on and on and on, steadily and ever so slowly pushing little gifts of new rocks and pebbles to the edge of the lake, each one made smooth as silk by the water itself. For a fleeting moment, one hot morning, as the humidity made itself more and more known with each passing minute, I thought that perhaps my baby would also love this lakeside. The thought was both terrifying and beautiful, and I destroyed it before I could dwell on it any longer.

That summer was hot; June had been gentle enough, but July came with ferocity. I began taking ice cold baths in the evening before bed. I felt the tiny being in my stomach jump from the cold.

My skin darkened into a light bronze. Late summer evenings were the best time of day; the world quieted down and, in the country, all but went away. The baby made me hot. Sometimes I would sleep most of the day until it began to cool in the early evening. I would go to the lake after dark when the sand had finally cooled and walk knee-deep through the water. I loved seeing the fluid, black crystal lake in the moonlight.

I saw Sonya every few weeks, and crying became inevitable during the counselling sessions. Was I softening? Ageing? Once as I sat down on Sonya's couch, I noticed that she had placed a brand-new box of Kleenex right beside a dwindling box of tissues. She planned on the tears.

Forest had hurt her paw during the summer and sported a bandage on her foot. She seemed embarrassed about the whole ordeal and would often tuck her foot underneath her stomach and wrap her tail around to cover all signs of the white bandage.

"You don't need to hide that, silly," I whispered to her one time as I was heading out Sonya's door.

And summer burned on. Time was as slow as frozen molasses in the moment, and yet it slipped by quickly. Like the tides, Time did not stop but moved relentlessly forward.

I was adrift, carried along.

XIV

I folded the soft cotton blanket neatly, slowly. Laundry had become a much larger task, more clothes to wash and more stains to scrub out. I carefully creased the little arm sleeves of a mint green jumper and set it beside several more piles of freshly washed baby clothes. I did not know which items I should keep and which I should give away.

The six to eight-month-old clothing did not need to be washed and most of them still had the tags attached. My baby would not be needing them because he was dead.

I gave birth to the baby on January fourth. One of the nurses handed the little purple and red body to me, and I held the soft baby against my chest. It was a boy. I brushed my index finger over the tight little fist.

"The woods are lovely, dark, and deep," I whispered in his ear so quietly that only he would hear me. "But I have promises to keep. And miles to go before I sleep, and miles to go before I sleep." His tiny mouth moved and curved into a yawn. I caught a glimpse of his rose petal tongue.

When asked what the baby's name would be, I said, "Miles."

"And middle name?"

I had to think. "Daniel, I suppose. For my dad."

My baby had died of SIDS. Sudden Infant Death Syndrome—the name so vague and ominous.

I had checked the clock: it read five, then six, then half-past six. Miles was soundly sleeping in his crib. Finally, the signs of a maturing baby. But when the clock passed seven, I had picked him up from the crib, my heart growing cold. I thought he would simply be jostled awake. The room was dark, the curtains were pulled shut to keep out the once bright sunshine that was now waning into dusk. My arms started shaking as I pulled his body away from my shoulder. I became distraught when I saw the frozen expression his face held, a lifeless cherub. He was entirely still.

I had called an ambulance. I followed the flashing lights that grew farther and farther away as cars pulled over for the ambulance and not me. I could barely see the road through the rivulets of tears rolling down my face. My mom tried to understand the words I spoke when I called, but she could only grasp that something was wrong with the baby and that I thought he was dead.

And I was right. Miles was dead upon arriving at the hospital, and every nurse, medic, and doctor in the vicinity cast the most sorrowful of expressions in my direction. Mom and Dad immediately drove the two hours to join me there. Mom had pushed chamomile lemon tea from the hospital cafeteria into my shaking hands.

I could not speak for a long time, and then I asked, *Did I do it? Did I do something wrong?* I knew I was unprepared, even with the many appointments at the pregnancy centre, even with all their pep talks and handouts. The unplanned pregnancy had been in the hands of an unplanned mother, and I had nervously laid awake at night wondering if I was forgetting something that would be crucial to the baby's development.

My parents had offered for me and the baby to stay with them as long as we needed, and so I stayed there for the first month after the birth. But I also needed my space and I didn't want to keep seeing my exhausted parents every morning, knowing that the baby and myself were the cause of the ashen crescents that curved around their eyes. I went back to my apartment and tried to manage the best I could, calling home with questions about feeding, bathing, sleep patterns, and a little patch of rash that ended up resolving itself. All of my senses were on hyper alert. The squirming in my arms, the muffled gurgles, the sharp cries, they all sent spikes of concern into my tired heart.

I resumed my regular dosage of clonazepam on the fifth day of January, the day after Miles's birth. My mind thawed slowly, a little more warmth found me. My low days were not as dangerously low, and a safeguard kept my emotions and thoughts from flying off the handle and into a dark oblivion.

One afternoon I had sat very still, Miles's silk lips pressed to my breast, intently feeding. The past nine months had looked so much like the weeks leading up to the day I'd swallowed the sixty-odd pills. The same bottomless blackness was present before I was rushed to the psych ward.

I lifted my hand to gently brush the tufts of dark hair on Miles's head. "You almost killed me," I whispered.

Jesse remained in his insulated world of insolence. I didn't hear much about him for several months. Someone said he had lost part of a finger in a work accident out west.

I had begun to think about the assault more. My consciousness had blocked it out, but it was seeping back, its serpent's tongue smelling the air for my scent, slithering back down the tree.

And then Miles died. And nihilism set in.

My mother's sister owned a cottage nestled on the edge of Lake Huron that was only accessible when snow and mud did not cover the dirt road that led to it. There were a handful of neighbouring cottages that branched off the same road, but besides them, it was a remote hamlet with no one else around. The aunt had said that I could stay at her cottage for a weekend, a week, however long I needed. Mom was nervous about the proposition, and probably debated on whether or not to relay her sister's offer to me. I would be grieving and alone, free to attempt suicide again. Her concern came far too late.

Dad asked that I call home once a day to assure them that I was all right. I agreed to this, packed a week's worth of clothing, and set off in the direction of the cottage.

I arrived at the small laneway to the little grey cottage on a Sunday afternoon. I set my bags down in the bedroom whose window faced the lake, then I sat down on the bed with a heavy sigh. After a few minutes I laid down on top of the bedspread, curled up into a tight crescent, and fell fast asleep.

I woke up disoriented and in the dark.

Silence—that's all there was. An all-encompassing silence that took up all the space between myself and the stars.

I turned on a lamp that shone weak, soft, lemon light and began to put the contents of my suitcase in the retro dresser.

I was hungry. I selected an almond granola bar and dried fruit—pineapple, ginger, apple—from the bag of non-perishable food items I had packed.

It was not cottage season yet. The early foggy mornings were deathly silent with no other cottagers in residency. I had walked as far north and south along the coastline as I could, and there was no sign of life. All the summer homes had shutters closed, sheds locked, Muskoka chairs covered in tarps. It was eerie, beautiful, supernatural.

One morning I froze in place as a loon descended upon the still lake water. It flew in alone, and no other loon joined it. The bird buoyed gently in place, deep scarlet-red eyes, black head, white paint flecks across the body. Its song was a long, haunting coo. As a young girl, they had always seemed otherworldly to me, as if a deep magic possessed them.

I watched the bird glide slowly across the water, poised and tranquil, alone on the lake. Staying fatefully still, I wondered if it were a male or female loon; I wondered where it had been born, where it had travelled, what knowledge it held—knowledge no human would ever know. Humanity was so capable, so knowledgeable, and yet did not know the things that a single loon knew.

The blood-red eyes turned toward the shoreline. I turned into a statue and the bird thought nothing of me. It quietly floated on the tranquil tides and I gazed after it until it took flight again.

I walked along the shoreline again, as I did every day since arriving at the cottage. The mind wandered far and wide during these walks. I felt slow and lethargic. I would think about Miles, my short-lived motherhood, and I would think about what to do with the years ahead of me. But more than anything, my childhood was brought to mind. Memories upon memories.

A short film rewound itself to the beginning and pressed play.

Smell of bird seed stored in the garage, wild raspberries growing unkempt in the yard, an ornate chandelier in the living room, chalk dust covering my bedroom floor after hours of playing teacher, the sound of blue jays squabbling in the maple tree outside the kitchen window, the chipmunk that couldn't find its way out of our garage for days, the never-once-lit candle that sat on the edge of the bathtub collecting dust, husking corn outside for dinner during hot summer evenings, plant germination experiments for the science fair, a rose stained glass window over the front door, toast cut up and dipped into maple syrup for breakfast, sand tracked throughout the house after an afternoon at the beach. Everything, everything.

Those memories were built into me, all so tangibly close, stored safely inside, and yet so distant and otherworldly, too long ago to be real.

The lake water remained smooth and unbothered by wind as it quietly rolled into the sandy shore. I craved a bitter cup of coffee and so I turned back toward the cottage.

There was a release when Miles died. A release of tears, a release of duty. Severance from a rapist. Jesse texted his condolences.

I went jogging in the morning and jogging in the evening. Two antonyms fought with demonic energy underneath my skin: solace and grief.

Miles died and I was no longer a mother and he was no longer the baby born of rape. A weight was lifted from both of us. Perhaps I sinned against Miles in feeling freed by his death. The grief was admirable, beautiful, a motherly hardship; the relief was vile, shocking, grotesque. Therefore, the grief was presented and the relief kept secret. The guilt of relief kept an even darker secret.

The funeral was small and the pastor kept his sermon concise. Jesse sat with his mother, both dripping in black. He was the assumed father, a broken father now, working out west for his loves, called back by the most unimaginable news. That is what every fellow mourner believed in their little broken hearts. I watched as they took in Jesse and myself, confused as to why we stood so far apart as the small coffin lowered.

Soon they would know; I would tell. I watched Jesse bow his head, unaware of what his future held.

The sand beneath my feet grew colder as the golden sun turned molten and melted into the horizon. Crickets resumed their nightly orchestra. I went indoors to find a sweater. When I returned to the shore, the sunset had shapeshifted into blood crimson, mellowing into a delicate pink where the light faded.

Acknowledgments

This book would not exist without Allison. My best friend. Our very first conversation, now over a decade ago, was about books, writing, and publishing. I would love to go back in time to talk to those two teenage girls and tell them, *you did it—yes, you.* I am proud of those two girls. Thank you so much for all the hard work and effort you poured into this book, and for editing my comma-ridden trains of thoughts. I love you.

Thank you, Natalie, for drowning all my woes in your kind encouragement and affirmation. Thank you for talking me down from all my little ledges. You listen to all my complaining and somehow still like me. It's kind of a miracle. Love you too.

Thank you, Cassie, for the beautiful cover design and for putting up with me in the process. Love you!

Twila Gingerich studied political science and peace and conflict at the University of Waterloo. When she's not writing, she works for a non-profit supporting individuals who have developmental disabilities. Twila grew up on the Bruce Peninsula but still calls it home.

This is Twila's first book. You can follow her at @twilagingerich and keep up with her future publications at @_elysianbooks.

Printed in Great Britain
by Amazon

42601497R00121